His kiss was fierce, firing her passion

He was in no hurry, exploring her lips, caressing her, making her tremble and shudder in his arms.

Suddenly he broke away, taking great gulps of air.

"Adam...." She was deeply bewildered.

"I could so easily have made love to you, Katy. We both wanted it. But would you have thanked me afterward? The repercussions of this morning could have changed your whole life."

"I wouldn't have let you do *that* to me!" she told him indignantly. "I-I could have stopped you. I had no intention of-of going all the way, of letting you appease your lust."

"My dear little Katy," Adam taunted, "You're wrong. You couldn't have stopped me if I'd decided to have you...."

CAROLE MORTIMER
is also the author of these

Harlequin Presents

Many of these titles are available at your local bookseller.

For a free catalogue listing all available Harlequin Romances
and Harlequin Presents, send your name and address to:

HARLEQUIN READER SERVICE
1440 South Priest Drive, Tempe, AZ 85281
Canadian address: Stratford, Ontario N5A 6W2

CAROLE MORTIMER

freedom to love

Harlequin Books

TORONTO • LONDON • LOS ANGELES • AMSTERDAM
SYDNEY • HAMBURG • PARIS • STOCKHOLM • ATHENS • TOKYO

Harlequin Presents edition published December 1981
ISBN 0-373-10473-3

Original hardcover edition published in 1981
by Mills & Boon Limited

CHAPTER ONE

KATY knew she had made a mistake about this holiday as soon as the plane took off from Heathrow. She was on her way to Calgary, one of Canada's fastest growing cities. She had wanted to see the country for so long that when Gemma and Gerald had suggested she accompany them she had jumped at the chance.

'But surely I'll just be in the way?' She had tried not to show her excitement.

'Probably,' agreed Gemma, her sister of twenty, the elder by two years, callously. 'But you know how old-fashioned Mum and Dad are. They'll never let Gerald and me go alone, even if we are getting married in a couple of years.'

Katy hadn't relished the idea of being taken along merely as a smoke-screen to her parents, and her reluctance must have shown.

'Oh, do come,' Gemma added persuasively. 'You know you'll love it out there.'

Canada beckoned, all that beautiful unspoilt country, and yet sharing it with Gemma and Gerald, her sarcastic boy-friend, didn't appeal at all.

'It's the only way you'll ever be able to go,' Gemma had told her cruelly. 'Your job as Dad's receptionist doesn't exactly pay well. Gerald and I will be paying for the camper, all you'll have to find is the money for your air fare and some spending money.'

'Only!' Katy scorned. 'Even that's out of my budget.'

'All right!' Gemma was becoming angry now, her green eyes narrowed. 'I'll help you pay for your air fare too, okay?'

Gemma must really have been desperate to have made such an offer, but Katy knew she could never accept it. 'I think I can just scrape through,' she refused the offer. 'If you really mean it about the camper?'

'Of course we do.' Gemma's eyes glowed now. 'You're an angel, Katy!'

That wasn't what her parents had called her when the idea was put to them. 'Oh, if Katy's going then that will be all right,' her father agreed unhesitantly to the idea. 'Katy's sensible. She'll see that no harm comes to you.'

Ever since she was a child Katy had been called the 'sensible' one, and she hated it! It wasn't even true. She was the one who at five had been playing 'Dare' with Gemma and had fallen off the diving-board at the local swimming-pool and had nearly drowned; she was the one who at ten had been balancing on the handlebars of Gemma's bicycle and had fallen off and knocked out her front teeth; she was the one who at sixteen had believed the married man who was giving her a lift home when he had told her he had run out of petrol as the car came to a halt on a deserted road. She was also the one who had ended up walking the five miles home when she realised his intention of seducing her.

And now here she was on this jumbo jet, setting out on an eight-and-a-half-hour flight to Canada when she hadn't ever flown before. Talk about going in at the deep end! And Gemma and Gerald didn't seem to give a damn about her welfare, totally engrossed in each other as they whispered and chatted together.

Katy was petrified, staring straight ahead as she felt the plane leave touch with the ground, her stomach seeming to be about four feet below the rest of her body and having great difficulty in catching up. Her fingers dug into the armrests; the one to her left seemed harder than the right.

She looked down to see her nails digging into the arm of the person sitting next to her, a definite male arm covered in faded denim. Oh no, she had done it again!

Her grey eyes slowly raised to meet the deepest blue eyes she had ever seen, the lashes thick and dark, as was the over-long hair, the skin a deep mahogany, the features seeming to be carved from granite. He was the hardest-looking man Katy had ever seen, possibly in his mid-thirties, those deep blue eyes the only redeeming feature against the hawk-like nose and firm forbidding mouth, the body lean and muscular, the denims he wore old and faded, matching the partly unbuttoned shirt he wore. He looked wealthy, despite the easy arrogance with which he wore the casual clothing, his whole bearing one of haughty assurance.

Katy realised she was still digging her nails into him. 'Sorry,' she quickly removed her hand, 'I didn't realise what I was doing.' She gave a nervous laugh. 'Silly to be frightened. I feel all right now.' And strangely enough she did; the plane seemed to be on an even keel, giving her stomach time to catch up with the rest of her body. 'I'm sorry about your arm. Did I hurt you?'

Blue eyes looked her over coldly for several long seconds, as if the man were surprised at her having spoken to him. 'No,' he answered finally, turning slightly in his seat, and if not actually turning his back on her giving a very good impression of it. He closed his eyes just for good measure.

Katy glared at him angrily. Rude, arrogant man! Digging her nails into him had been an accident, the least he could have done was acknowledge her apology. And yet by the look of the even rise and fall of that wide muscular chest, he had already fallen asleep. She felt dismissed by an expert.

She unfastened her seat belt when told to do so, accepting the orange juice the air hostess brought round minutes later, knowing her stomach was still too shaky to take the alcohol offered.

The air hostess looked at the sleeping man at Katy's side. 'Would your husband care for a drink, do you think?' she asked her politely.

Katy flushed, glancing nervously at the face that appeared cold and hard even in sleep. 'Er—I—I'm not——'

Suddenly the man sat up, moving with quiet grace and favouring the air hostess with a slow sensual smile, his eyes appreciating her slim beauty. 'I'll have a Scotch, thanks. And just for the record, I'm not her husband. I'm not her father either,' he drawled, his voice as English as Katy's own, only more so, indicating a private schooling.

'Sorry about the mistake, sir.' The air hostess gave him a dazzling smile back and handed him his drink before going on to the next row.

He turned to look at Katy. 'Well?' he quirked one dark eyebrow.

She blushed as she realised she was staring at him, watching in amazement as he drank the whisky straight down without even a wince. The first and only time she had ever tried the spirit it had seemed to burn all the way down to her stomach.

'Sorry,' she mumbled, turning away and pretending an interest in the rather silly lovers' talk Gemma and Gerald were indulging in. They had been served by another hostess on their side, and it appeared that as they were sitting in a row of four seats Katy would continue to be grouped with the arrogant stranger at her side all during the flight.

As they had taken off just after midday it wasn't long before they were being served lunch, but the man at Katy's side only opened his eyes long enough to refuse his meal. Katy had to admit she was a little piqued by his attitude. Okay, so she was a little young for him to interest himself in, but she wasn't exactly unattractive.

Her hair was what Gemma cattily called the colour of fudge, although she preferred to say caramel-coloured, her eyes wide and grey, her nose small and to her relief, unfreckled, her mouth wide and smiling. Her complexion was good too now, the hated teenage spots had seemed to fade the year before, as had her puppy fat, leaving her tall and slender.

Perhaps this man would prefer to sleep than eat the food, although Katy didn't think it anything like the cardboard food she had been led to expect; it was in fact quite enjoyable. Or maybe this man was just trying to cut down on calories, perhaps that was how he managed to stay lean and firmly muscled when most men his age would be well on their way to middle-aged spread. Whatever his reason his eyes stayed firmly closed as those around him ate their meal, the first excited chatter beginning to die down as the long flight stretched in front of them all.

Once again the man at her side seemed to know when the drinks were being brought round, although this time he opted for coffee, several cups of it, black. The air hostess, a girl probably in her late twenties, returned to him again and again to see if he required anything else. And by the invitation in her eyes she clearly meant *anything*.

Katy pointedly ignored the man, although this left her fairly isolated, shut out by her sister and Gerald, and determined not to even notice the man on her other side. She was glad therefore when the film came on the screen in front of her, a screen that appeared to be the back of the painting that had recently been displayed there. She had hired the earphones from the air hostess at the start of the flight, intending to listen to the radio later, but the film would be much more interesting. Besides, it would take up a couple of hours of the flight.

The film was one that had recently toured the cinemas, one that she hadn't had the time to go and see. It looked strange without the necessary sound. She looked down for the place to plug in her ear-phones, realising she should have thought to do it before the window-blinds were lowered and the lights dimmed. Where on earth was the hole for the other end of her earphones?

Impatient fingers pushed her hand away as she sought frantically for the right place, dealing with the plugging in within a matter of seconds. Katy looked up shyly to thank the man she had so far thought rude and arrogant.

He was watching her with narrowed eyes, eyes that no longer seemed deeply blue but were glacial. 'Are you always this helpless?' he asked contemptuously.

She flushed. 'I——'

'Don't bother,' he impatiently dismissed her reply. 'Just watch your film. Maybe then I'll be able to get some rest without your fidgeting about beside me.'

'I wasn't fidgeting!' Katy told him indignantly, looking about them almost guiltily as she realised other people could hear this conversation. Luckily no one was listening, all seemingly engrossed in the film, and so all other sound was blocked out. 'Anyway,' she added resentfully, 'you've been sleeping since we left London.'

'Sorry!' His sarcasm was blatantly obvious. 'I wasn't aware I was here to entertain you.'

'You aren't,' she blushed.

'Thank God for that!' He leant his dark head back, closing his eyes again. 'Idiotic females, particularly young ones, bore me silly.'

'Ooh!' Her mouth set mutinously.

He opened one eye to look at her. 'Shut you up?'

'Yes!' Katy snapped.

'Good.' He smiled, closing his eyes again.

Well, really! Katy stuck the ear-phones on, turning the sound down as it roared into her eardrums. For all the notice she took of the film, or the dialogue, she might just as well not have bothered. She was too angry and upset to concentrate on anything at the moment. This man must have taken lessons on how to be unpleasant, he was so good at it.

She shot him a resentful glance, having to admit an unwilling attraction to his dark good looks. It was probably his looks that enabled him to be this high-handed with her; most people, particularly women, would forgive him anything. So might she have done if he had turned the charming smile on her that he had given the air hostess. But he had decreed her too young for his attention, and had dismissed her from his mind accordingly.

The film was almost halfway through when she realised her orange juice and after-lunch coffee were taking their toll on her. She could see the sign for the toilets; the only trouble was, she couldn't get out. Gemma and Gerald were engrossed in the film and wouldn't thank her for disturbing them, and the sleeping man at her side would thank her even less.

After another half an hour of moving restlessly about in her seat, giving up any attempt to concentrate on the film, she was feeling desperate. She *had* to get up, the question was whose wrath was she going to evoke by asking them to let her out.

'For God's sake, woman!' the man at her side exploded, sitting upright in his seat to glare at her with angry blue eyes. 'Don't you know how to sit still?'

'Of course I do!' Katy was angry herself now, having put up with his boorishness long enough. 'But it isn't easy when you want to go to the loo!' She blushed at having to talk about such intimacies to this stranger.

'Why the hell didn't you just say so?' he snapped, already beginning to stand up to let her pass.

She drew a deep angry breath. 'Maybe because I knew this would be your reaction. You are without doubt the rudest man I've ever met!' With this comment she flounced off.

Her bravado lasted her as long as it took her to reach the privacy of the toilets, staying there much longer than she needed to because she dreaded returning to her seat. She took her time over renewing her make-up and tidying her hair, finally bracing herself to go back and face that awful man.

The blinds had been lifted and the lights were fully back on, and people were wandering about the plane talking to each other. Kate almost heaved a sigh of relief as she saw the seat next to hers was empty.

'What's his name?' Her sister turned to look at her.

Katy looked startled. 'Whose?'

Gemma gave her an impatient look. 'The man sitting next to you. I'm sure I've seen him somewhere before. Gerald thinks he has too.'

Now she came to think of it he did look slightly familiar, although she felt sure she wouldn't have forgotten him if she had ever met him before. He wasn't the sort of man you could forget! 'Why should I know his name?' she asked tersely.

'You seem to have been talking to him.'

Talking? What they had been doing certainly couldn't be called talking, it was more like an argument. 'A few casual words,' she evaded. 'Nothing as revealing as names.'

'Yours wouldn't reveal much,' Gemma scorned, turning back to her boy-friend.

Charming! Katy was surrounded by them. She had

even been dismissed as a nonentity by her sister now. She was getting a definite feeling of rejection.

The long length of her arrogant stranger coiled down into the seat next to her and she forced herself not to even look at him. She wasn't risking any more rebuffs from him. She stared rigidly down at the paperback in her hand, not taking in a word of it.

'You aren't safe to be let out on your own,' that silky voice taunted as he bent to retrieve something off the floor. 'Here,' he held out her purse to her. 'It is yours, I presume?'

Katy paled, almost snatching it out of his hand. All her money was in here, all her travellers cheques. The only things she had kept separate were her passport and her return air ticket. 'Thank you,' she said breathlessly. 'I— It must have fallen out when I got my book out.'

'Obviously,' he said dryly. 'Is someone meeting you at the other end?' he added thoughtfully.

Her eyes widened. 'I beg your pardon?'

Her reaction seemed to amuse him. 'I wasn't propositioning you. But you don't appear to be safe to let cross the road, let alone the Atlantic,' he said insultingly.

'No one is meeting me,' she answered stiltedly. 'I happen to be going to Canada on holiday—with my sister and her boy-friend. They're sitting the other side of me,' she added at his sceptical look.

He glanced around her, sitting back with a shrug. 'She's nothing like you to look at.'

Katy knew that, had always known that Gemma was the beautiful one of the family. Gemma was honey-blonde where she was caramel, had deep green eyes where Katy's were grey, and her sister had never been troubled by spots or puppy fat, seeming to the younger Katy to have always been slim and petite.

'I know that,' she snapped at this man. 'But that doesn't

make it any less a fact that she is my sister.'

'Prickly little thing, aren't you?' he taunted. 'Rather like the wild rose the Canadians are so fond of.'

'Are they?' Katy frowned.

'Mm,' he nodded. 'Especially where we're going. Alberta is its home. It's very common up there on the mountains just below the timberline.'

'Timberline?' she echoed dazedly.

'Tut, tut, tut,' he mocked, seemingly fully awake now, and even more taunting than he had been before. 'You haven't done your homework on Alberta. I take it you intend touring the National Parks there?'

'Yes,' she nodded.

'Then you should know that the timberline is where it becomes too cold up in the mountains for the trees to survive, they just suddenly stop growing, hence the term timberline. Make sense?' he quirked an eyebrow questioningly.

'Oh yes,' her eyes glowed. 'Thank you.'

'Don't mention it,' he dismissed. 'Your name wouldn't happen to be Rose?'

She shook her head. 'Katy—Katy Harris.'

'Shame. Rose suits you so much better.'

'I don't think so,' she said crossly. 'I don't consider it prickly just because I don't like your taunting behaviour.'

'Was I taunting you?' He sounded amused again.

'You know you were.'

'Maybe.' He frowned. 'Where's your boy-friend?'

She flushed. 'I don't have one,' she told him resentfully.

'No? So it's just a cosy little threesome, is it?'

'I don't like your implication,' Katy snapped. 'Gemma and Gerald are engaged to be married. It was very kind of them to invite me on this holiday with them.' She knew that kindness hadn't entered into it, but she wasn't about to tell this man that.

'Gemma and Gerald!' he taunted mockingly. 'How nice.'

'God, you're sarcastic!' She turned her back on him, hearing his throaty chuckle behind her.

What an unpleasant creature he was! But how dangerously attractive, with that wicked gleam of amusement in his blue eyes, albeit cruel amusement.

'You lucky devil,' Gemma told her in a fierce whisper. 'Gerald and I have just realised who you're sitting next to,' she explained at Katy's puzzled look. 'Well, Gerald realised it first,' she grudgingly admitted.

'Well?' Katy asked patiently.

'He's Adam Wild!' Gemma announced triumphantly.

'Don't be ridiculous,' Katy instantly dismissed the idea. 'He would be in the first class, not back here with the rabble.' Adam Wild was the top photographer in England, usually specialising in photographs of beautiful women, both clothed and unclothed. He was also rich enough not to have to travel in economy class.

Gemma scowled. 'Maybe there weren't any first class seats left. Anyway, you were talking to him for some time just now, didn't he tell you his name?'

'It wasn't that sort of conversation.'

Her sister sighed. 'Trust you to miss an opportunity like that! Well, if he talks to you again find out if we're right.'

'I don't intend talking to him again. I don't like him.'

Gemma gave her a pitying look before turning away, and Katy knew she had gone down even further in her sister's estimation. But surely this man couldn't be Adam Wild? He was dressed so casually, for one thing, and as she had pointed out to Gemma, he was hardly likely to be sitting here.

Minutes later the air hostess came round with their

afternoon tea, and Katy gratefully accepted the refreshing cup of tea that went with the light fare. She almost dropped her cup as she heard the girl call the man at her side 'Mr Wild', and as it was she spilt some of the hot liquid over her denims. It *was* him—Adam Wild!

She looked at him with new eyes, seeing the lines of dissipation and cynicism beside his nose and mouth, the worldly air that encircled him despite his casual clothing. God, no wonder he had coldly dismissed her; she was passably attractive, but the women he photographed were beautiful and sophisticated.

'It's soaking into your denims,' he turned to her to remark patiently.

'I—I beg your pardon?' Katy jumped nervously as he spoke.

'Your tea—you're spilling it all over you.' He took her cup out of her unresisting fingers and began mopping her up with his paper napkin. 'Couldn't you feel it dripping down on you?' he asked, as if she were a particularly stupid child.

'I—er——' She licked her lips nervously, completely overwhelmed as he touched the inside of her thigh, purely to mop up the liquid, of course. 'Yes,' she nodded vigorously.

He shook his head. 'Then why the hell didn't you stop doing it?'

'I—I—You see, Mr Wild, I——'

'Ah,' he nodded understanding, 'you know who I am.'

'I heard the air hostess,' she confirmed, wishing he would stop touching her like that.

'And you would like to take your clothes off for me.' He finally sat back, discarding the tissue paper with a certain amount of disgust.

'Certainly not!' Katy gasped.

He studied her critically for several minutes. 'You'll

never make it on the face alone. The bone structure is good, but it isn't enough on its own. The clothes would have to come off. I'm sure that under that loose shirt and denims there's a beautiful body just waiting to show itself.'

'And I'm sure there's no such thing!' she told him indignantly, the totally assessing look in his eyes making her feel like wrapping her arms protectively about herself. 'I'm not taking my clothes off for you or any other man!'

'Why not?'

'Why not? Because—well, because I—I don't even know you!'

Once again he seemed amused by her. 'What difference does that make? I think you could be very photogenic. Are your eyes really grey or is it my imagination?'

'They're grey,' she snapped confirmation.

'A lovely smoky grey. And hair the colour of toffee.'

'Caramel!' Katy corrected crossly.

He shrugged. 'Okay, caramel. And there's a beautiful body under all those clothes, right?'

'Mind your own business!'

'Beautiful bodies, female ones, *are* my business.' He pulled a card out of his denim shirt pocket and handed it to her. 'When you get back to London give me a call and we'll try some practice sesssions.'

'Practising for what?' she asked spitefully.

His mouth hardened, his eyes glacial. 'I'm thirty-six years old, give me sense enough not to chase after schoolgirls!'

'I'm not a schoolgirl. I'm eighteen.'

'Wow!' he taunted sarcastically, picking up the card she had put on the arm of his seat and bending forward to put the card down the open vee of her shirt, leaving it nestling between her breasts. 'If the rest of you looks as good as they feel,' he removed his hand, 'then I think I may be able to put some work your way.'

'You can keep your work!' She took out the card and
ripped it into tiny pieces in front of him before putting it
in the ashtray. 'And anything else you have to offer.'

'Okay,' he shrugged. 'If that's the way you want it.'

'It is,' she told him firmly.

She didn't know whether she was relieved or not when
he finally seemed to fall asleep again. Her thoughts were
much too chaotic for her to even attempt to sleep herself.
No man had ever touched her so intimately, and especially
so publicly. Colour flooded her cheeks as she remembered his suggestion that he photograph her nude.

'Well?' Gemma turned to her expectantly.

Katy didn't even pretend not to know what her sister
meant. 'You were right, it is him.'

'I thought so!' Gemma's eyes sparkled excitedly. 'What
did he give you just now?'

It had been too much to hope that Gemma hadn't seen
that interchange! 'Just his card,' Katy revealed reluctantly.

'*Just* his card?' her sister repeated dazedly. 'And did I
see you rip it up?'

'You did. I have no desire to be photographed in the
nude.'

Gemma spluttered with laughter. 'He wanted to
photograph *you*?'

'My body,' Katy corrected disgustedly, his remark that
she would never make it on her face alone still rankling.

'And you turned him down?'

'Of course I did,' she said crossly. 'I told you, I don't
want him photographing me.' She didn't like his totally
analytical gaze, didn't like the way he had dismissed her
face and instead assessed her body as photographable. She
pitied his wife if he had one—how awful to be stripped
down to the bare bone, so to speak. After all, no one was

perfect, and this man was more than qualified to pick out any blemish or imperfection. 'Besides,' she added, 'you know it isn't possible. And Mum and Dad would never allow it.'

'If Adam Wild wanted to photograph me I wouldn't let Mum and Dad stop me,' Gemma said scornfully.

'And Gerald?' Katy asked dryly.

'It wouldn't bother me.' He sat forward to answer for himself. 'I might get quite a kick out of seeing *my* girl-friend's picture in a centrefold.'

It was the sort of stupid remark Katy would have expected from him. Despite his fair good looks, Katy had always considered Gerald one of the silliest men she knew. Part of her dislike could be due to the fact that he had first started dating Gemma when Katy was going through the worst of her puppy fat and spots stage, and he had never forgotten it. He had teased her unmercifully then, his barbs often cruel and hurtful, and he still did so, every chance he could. Katy stayed away from him whenever she could.

'Gemma didn't get the offer,' she reacted strongly to him. 'And *I* have no intention of taking it up.'

Gerald's brown eyes passed over her scornfully. 'I can't see what the man saw in you,' and he turned away.

'Idiot!' Gemma snapped at her resentfully, before she too turned away.

'Tell him I have a thing about firm uptilted breasts,' remarked a soft taunting voice from next to Katy.

She spun round, her eyes wide with indignation. 'What did you say?' she gasped.

Adam Wild gave her a lazy smile, a completely relaxed look about him as he slouched down in his seat. 'I like nicely rounded bottoms too,' he added outrageously. 'So you pass on both counts.'

Katy glared at him. 'How do you know that?'

'I watched you as you walked to the loo,' he informed her calmly. 'I've always thought tight denims a good figure revealer. Of course, I couldn't see your legs, but——'

'Leave my legs out of it!' she said fiercely.

'But I'm sure they're equally curvaceous,' he continued as if she hadn't spoken.

'How awful to look at every woman through the eyes of a camera,' Katy snapped, 'to always see the faults. I pity your wife,' she voiced her thoughts of a few minutes ago.

Adam Wild gave a throaty chuckle, suddenly appearing younger than his thirty-six years. 'I'm not married, Katy,' he said with humour. 'And never likely to be.'

'Too choosy, I suppose,' she said insultingly, surprised at her own vehemence towards this man. She didn't normally take violent dislikes to people.

'Too much choice,' he told her insinuatingly. 'There are too many girls only too eager to give their all if I'll photograph them. Sometimes I take them up on that offer. So you see, I don't always see the faults.'

Katy hated the way those deep blue eyes were laughing at her. 'Tell me, Mr Wild, why are you sitting back here with us lesser mortals? Wouldn't you have been more comfortable up the front with your own sort?' Her sarcasm was unmistakable.

'Miss Harris,' his voice was deceptively mild, his eyes no longer laughing, 'until the general public decided to take me to their bosoms about fifteen years ago, I belonged with the "lesser mortals". And that was your description, not mine,' he added hardly. 'Besides, what does it matter where I sit when all I want to do is rest?'

'I suppose that's because you took one of those girls up on their offer last night!'

His eyes suddenly appeared flinty grey, and Katy wondered how she had ever thought them a deep blue. 'I'm not so old that a night of love physically exhausts me,' he told her harshly. 'I just don't happen to have slept for seventy-two hours.'

'*Three* nights of love!' she taunted.

'Miss Harris, go jump in a lake,' he said calmly.

Katy was prevented from answering by the sudden request to fasten seat belts, and the dropping of the aeroplane as they approached Calgary. She had that terrible feeling in her stomach again, only this time it was worse. Her nails dug into the arm-rest, luckily not Adam Wild's arm this time, but her panic just seemed to be getting worse.

She heard an impatient sigh beside her and a male hand, palm upwards, came into her vision. She didn't stop to think that this was Adam Wild offering her comfort, that he was the man she had taken an instant dislike to; all that mattered right now was that he understood how she felt and was trying to help her.

Her hand crept into his much larger one, his long tapered fingers closing about hers. His thumb rubbed rhythmically over the back of her hand, soothing away some of her panic and making her feel secure when moments ago she had felt near to hysteria.

'Thank you,' she said huskily once they had come to a standstill outside the airport building. 'I—Thank you,' she repeated weakly.

'Don't mention it.' Already he was standing up to depart. 'I won't ask any payment for it, so you can stop looking worried.'

Colour flooded her cheeks. 'I didn't think you would! And I wasn't looking worried.'

'Then perhaps you ought to,' he remarked with humour. 'Your sister and her boy-friend have just departed down the other aisle.'

Katy turned startled grey eyes to see he was in fact correct. Gemma and Gerald hadn't even told her they were going, and now they were almost out of the plane. She scrambled to her feet, almost falling over in her panic.

A hand came out to grasp her elbow. 'Calm down,' Adam Wild advised her. 'They won't have got far. It usually takes some time to get through Customs. Come on,' he pulled her out into the aisle beside him, 'I'll take you through.'

'There's no need——'

'There's every need,' he insisted. 'During our brief acquaintance I've come to realise that you're incapable of doing anything without something going wrong.'

'That isn't true——'

'I don't have the time to argue, Katy. Nearly everyone else is off the plane. Now, come on.'

Katy let herself be led towards the exit, furious with her sister and Gerald for leaving her at the mercy of this sarcastic man.

The air hostess who had served them during their flight was standing at the doorway. 'I hope you both enjoyed your flight,' she smiled at them both, although the smile was brighter as her gaze rested on Adam Wild. 'I hope you weren't too uncomfortable, Mr Wild. I'm sorry there were no first class seats available.'

'That's all right,' he returned the smile with lazy charm. 'I just needed a seat, I didn't care where.' He manoeuvred Katy so that they departed together, striding along and pulling her with him.

'So you did try to get in first class,' she accused in a fierce whisper.

He shrugged. 'I tried.'

'You do realise that the hostess was one of those girls making an offer,' Katy scorned, having trouble keeping up with his pace, but the hand on her arm not allowing her to lag behind.

'Too flat-chested,' he dismissed callously. 'A beautiful face, charming manner, but no bust.'

Katy became angry for the other girl. 'How would you like it if you were discarded because you had too little— too little——' She couldn't think of a male equivalent, at least, not one she could say to this man!

He looked down at her, one eyebrow arched mockingly. 'Too little . . .?' he prompted tauntingly.

'If you were found lacking!' she amended crossly.

He shrugged. 'I've had no complaints so far,' he told her calmly.

'Well, really!' Katy pulled away from him to join one of the queues of people waiting to pass through the Canadian passport control.

She was immediately pulled out of the queue to stand beside Adam Wild. 'Not that one,' he told her. 'Not unless you have a Canadian passport. You don't, do you?'

'You know I don't!' She glared at him with angry grey eyes.

'Then you won't get very far standing there. It happens to be for Canadian citizens only.'

'Well, I didn't know that!'

'You do now.' He looked down at her. 'What hotel are you staying at in Calgary?'

She eyed him suspiciously. 'Why?'

'So that I know which area to avoid on my way through.' He gave a throaty chuckle at the indignation on her face. 'You have to admit, you're a bit of a disaster.'

'I admit no such thing. Just because I've made a few mistakes——'

'A few!' he scorned. 'You can't seem to do anything without getting into trouble.'

'I can,' she defended. 'But this is my first time on an

aeroplane. I was nervous, frightened on occasion,' she said with remembered embarrassment. 'I think that's ample excuse for those few mistakes I made.'

He shook his head impatiently. 'Your first time in the air and you choose to fly to Canada!' He gave her a scathing glance. 'You could have been sick for the whole of the flight. I suppose I would have had to cope with that too,' he finished disgustedly.

'I didn't ask for your help. I could have managed perfectly well on my own.'

'Oh sure,' he scorned. 'You're the epitome of cool efficiency.'

Hot colour entered her creamy cheeks. 'And you're the arrogant bighead I would have expected you to be! Just because I'm a little inexperienced about dealing with airport officials and——'

'Inexperienced!' he mocked. 'You're like a babe in arms. And it looks as if your sister has already gone through. Will she wait for you?'

'Of course she will!' Katy was still angered by her sister's desertion of her. Some holiday this was going to be if Gemma and Gerald were going to keep leaving her out like this!

'I hope so,' the man at her side said grimly, 'because I simply don't have the time to help you out of another disaster. I'm being met.'

'You have friends in Canada?'

'A few,' he nodded.

'Female friends,' she said knowingly.

'Some,' Adam Wild smiled.

'Will she mind my being with you?'

'She——? Oh, I'm not being met by a she, Katy. And I'm sure Jud won't mind seeing you with me, in fact he'll probably enjoy it.'

'I see.'

'Disappointed?' he bent his head to whisper against her earlobe. 'Would you have enjoyed being the cause of trouble between a girl-friend and myself?'

'I might have done.' Katy's head was back challengingly.

He shook his head, smiling. 'Why on earth you were blessed with such tranquil grey eyes I'll never know. They're at complete variance with your stormy nature.'

'I don't have a stormy nature,' she snapped, immediately contradicting the statement. Blushing, she turned away.

Once they had shown their passports and collected their luggage, Katy's brand new case, and Adam Wild's battered holdall, they made their way outside to the curiously empty airport.

A tall man with deep red hair and laughing blue eyes detached himself from several people standing outside and made his way towards the man standing confidently at Katy's side.

'Adam!' He shook his friend's hand with unconcealed pleasure. 'Glad you could get back so quickly.' His accent was distinctly Canadian.

Adam grinned at him. 'I always like to finish what I start. God protect me from jealous women!' He grimaced.

Jud turned to look pointedly at Katy. 'This isn't——'

Adam laughed. 'Good God, no!'

'In that case . . . I'm Jud Turner,' he introduced himself to Katy.

She couldn't help returning the open friendliness of this man. 'Katy Harris,' she divulged shyly, still wondering what Adam Wild had meant by his remark about 'jealous women'. Jud Turner obviously knew the answer because he hadn't questioned the remark. She turned to Adam Wild, her smile instantly fading. 'Thank you for your— help,' she said reluctantly, politeness calling for some acknowledgement of the assistance he had given her. 'If you'll both excuse me, I have to join my sister.'

Adam nodded. 'Take care, Katy,' he advised with ill-concealed humour. He took another of his cards out of the breast pocket of his denim shirt. 'Don't tear this one up,' he warned. 'Call me when you get back to London.' He put the card in exactly the same place as he had the first one.

Katy's cheeks flamed, and she would have liked to have slapped that taunting smile off his face. Instead she removed the card and with one last glance in Adam Wild's direction she walked off, her head held high.

'Pretty girl,' she heard Jud Turner remark.

'Passable,' Adam Wild drawled. 'It wasn't her face I was interested in.'

'It never is,' his friend returned.

Katy heard the two men laugh together and anger flared within her. So she was just a body to Adam Wild, just a faceless piece of flesh and bones that he thought photographable. God, she hated him!

CHAPTER TWO

GEMMA and Gerald were waiting outside the airport building. Well, at least they hadn't gone on to the hotel without her!

'Do hurry up, Katy,' her sister snapped. 'We've been waiting ages for you.'

She didn't think five minutes constituted 'ages', but she wasn't going to start an argument in the middle of Calgary airport. 'Mr Wild was just helping——'

Gemma sighed, interrupting her. 'You've been talking to him again!' It was almost an accusation.

'Did you take him up on his offer?' Gerald wanted to know.

Katy gave him a contemptuous glare, wondering how she could have let herself in for two weeks of this unbearable man's company. She would just have to try and keep out of his way as much as possible, otherwise there were going to be a few heated arguments before the end of this holiday.

'Don't be silly, Gerald,' Gemma giggled as she held on to his arm. 'Katy's too much of a prude to take her clothes off for any man.'

Hot colour flooded Katy's cheeks, and out of the corner of her eyes she saw Adam Wild and Jud Turner leaving the airport, their avid conversation showing that she had long been forgotten. 'There's a time and place for everything,' she told them stiffly. 'And in front of a camera, before a complete stranger, is neither the time or the place.'

'Oh, we know the right place,' Gemma gazed up adoringly at Gerald. 'Don't we, darling?'

'You bet!' he grinned down at her.

Katy was feeling decidedly in the way. Surely they weren't going to behave like this all the holiday, making her feel completely unwanted. 'Shall we get a taxi?' she suggested brightly.

She sat quietly in the corner during the drive to the hotel, finding it strange being driven on the right-hand side of the road. The landscape was very flat from the airport to the hotel they were booked into overnight, and Katy felt misgivings for the beautiful scenery she had expected to see. But perhaps it changed when you got a few miles out of Calgary; the scenery around Heathrow wasn't exactly encouraging either.

The hotel was quietly comfortable, its decor like one of the older hotels in London rather than the modernness she had expected. But Katy preferred it, looking about her admiringly while Gerald went to the reception to see about their rooms. The hotel and camper had all been arranged through an agency in England, and so far it all seemed to be running smoothly. The people who hired out the camper insisted that anyone from abroad spend one night in a hotel in order to get over the long flight out here. It seemed a sensible idea to Katy.

'Ready?' Gerald was dangling the keys in front of them, summoning the lift. 'We're on the seventh floor and you're on the tenth, Katy,' he told her.

She followed them dazedly into the lift. 'I—You——'

He spluttered with laughter. 'I do believe our Katy thought she was to share a room with you, Gemma,' he grinned down at his fiancée.

'Did you?' Gemma snuggled into Gerald's arms. Katy's pale face gave her her answer. 'Do grow up, Katy,' she scorned. 'Gerald and I have been sleeping together for almost two years now, and we certainly don't intend to sleep apart here. The single room was always intended for you.'

This was getting worse and worse. Katy had had an idea that Gerald and her sister had slept together in the past, but to use her as a shield like this was deplorable. Not that she was the prude her sister had accused her of being; she just didn't like being used to dupe her parents. Her father had even helped pay her airfare, saying the experience of seeing Canada would be good for her. Poor innocent Mum and Dad, they could have had no idea of Gemma and Gerald's plans.

'See you later,' said Gemma as the lift stopped at the seventh floor and she and Gerald stepped out. 'Come down about seven and we'll all go down to dinner together.'

'I think I'll eat in my room and then get an early night.' Katy ignored Gerald's self-satisfied smile, her anger almost at exploding point.

Gemma sighed. 'You aren't going to sulk, are you?'

'Certainly not,' she said stiffly, pressing the button for her own floor. 'I'll see you in the morning,' she had time to say before the doors closed.

Really, this was just too much! She had always thought Gerald a louse, but she had expected better of Gemma. She was helping to make an absolute fool of her, and Katy wished it were possible for her to go home. But it wasn't, and it was a childish thought. She would just have to weather this out and hope that the two weeks went quickly. But she felt lonely already.

Her room was pleasant, having quite a nice view over the towering buildings of Calgary. It was a well-laid-out room, not big, but with everything she could possibly need, including an adjoining bathroom. There was a single bed against one wall, a small table and chairs near the window, an armchair in front of the colour television set that stood on half the desk. Yes, it was all very comfortable, but right now all Katy wanted to do was fall asleep.

It seemed no sooner had her head touched the soft downy pillow than she was asleep, a dreamless sleep that didn't seem to have refreshed her at all when she woke a few hours later. It was five o'clock here, which meant it was twelve o'clock at night in England, and her body didn't seem to have caught up with her, leaving her feeling slightly numb.

She switched on the television, but the vast choice of channels threw her. She was used to only three at home, with a fourth one in the making, and here she seemed to have twelve channels. Not all of them were showing something, but there was enough to make the choice difficult.

She lay down on the bed to study the room-service menu, determined not to see her sister and Gerald until she felt more able to face the situation they had put her in. A sandwich would do fine, she could always have something else later if she felt like it. And a pot of tea. How she would love a pot of tea!

The order phoned down, and the possibility of a slight wait according to the girl on the switchboard, Katy decided to have a refreshing shower. Maybe then she would start to feel more human. It was certainly turning out to be a long day; the seven-hour time difference had thrown her completely.

What was Adam Wild doing now? No doubt he and his friend had looked up a couple of the female friends Adam Wild claimed to have here, and were now enjoying themselves. She sorted through her handbag, taking out the card he had given her. It was just his name and telephone number, printed starkly in bold black letters. No frills or fancy lettering for this man. She would keep the card, keep it as a memento of her meeting with the famous Adam Wild.

Katy lay back again, once again seeing that hard cynical face, the mocking blue eyes, the lean sensual body. Many women must have known the possession of that body, and yet none of them had ever possessed the man, and she doubted any woman ever would. Adam Wild had the look of the eternal bachelor.

She pushed him to the back of her mind as her sandwich arrived, wishing now that she had thought to dress, conscious of the young boy's gaze roaming over her robe-covered body. The tea was very welcome, the club sandwich she had ordered a meal in itself. Goodness, she had never seen such a sandwich, tomato, bacon, thick slices of beef, all layered between several slices of bread.

A quiz programme came on the television, and she sat and watched it as she ate, not bothering to dress now. It was already seven-thirty, and she would be going to bed in a moment.

She jumped nervously as the telephone rang, knowing it must be Gemma and Gerald. She had only just begun to relax, and could well do without their taunting. 'Yes?' she spoke coldly into the receiver.

'Katy?'

Her heart fluttered at the sound of that deep husky voice with the sexual undertones. Adam Wild! She would recognise his voice anywhere. 'Yes?' she asked suspiciously.

'Adam here,' she could almost hear the humour in his voice. 'Adam Wild,' he supplied unnecessarily. And he knew it was unnecessary, damn him. 'Come down and have dinner with me,' he invited.

'You're in the hotel?' She couldn't contain her surprise.

'In reception,' he confirmed. 'I just saw your sister and her boy-friend going in to dinner, so I know you're alone.'

'Taking pity on me once again, Mr Wild?' she snapped angrily.

'And if I am?'

'It isn't necessary,' she told him distantly. 'I've already eaten. I'm just about to go to bed.' A slight exaggeration, but it wouldn't be too long before she went back to bed, she felt very tired.

He gave a husky laugh. 'If that's an invitation, I accept.'

'It wasn't,' Katy snapped. 'Now, if you'll excuse me . . .'

'Is that any way to treat me, Katy Harris?' His voice had hardened.

'When you've just invited yourself into my bed it is. What happened to your friend?'

'Jud? He had business elsewhere.'

'Look, I'm sorry, Mr Wild, but——'

'If you don't come down, Katy,' he interrupted softly, 'I'm likely to come up there. Do you want that?'

'No!'

'Well?'

'All right,' she said crossly. 'You go ahead and have your dinner and I'll meet you in—say, an hour.'

'Fine,' he agreed briskly. 'Don't be late,' he warned before ringing off.

She wouldn't dare, not with the threat of him coming to her room. How had he found her? More to the point, *why* had he found her?

She dressed with care, wearing one of the only two dresses she had brought with her, deciding that denims and tops were more practical for the type of holiday they were on. But as they were staying two nights at this hotel, once this evening and once on the eve of their departure, she had brought two dresses with her. Thank goodness she had; she had the feeling Adam Wild expected sophistication from his companions.

Her dress was chocolate brown, below knee-length, with a fitted bodice and pencil-thin skirt, with a slit up one side of the skirt so that she could walk without hindrance. It was quite a daring dress, very figure-hugging, but the other one was even more so, the bodice on that one consisting of a thin wisp of material held up by two very thin shoulder-straps. At least the brown dress covered her body, even if it did outline every curve!

Her hair she brushed loosely down her back, completely straight, held back from her face by two thin slides at her temples. Her make-up was light, just a light touch of brown eyeshadow and mascara, with a peach lip-gloss on her mouth. She felt satisfied with the result, feeling cool and self-assured.

That coolness and assurance disappeared as soon as Adam Wild's warm gaze slid over her with slow assessment, reducing her to the blushing young girl that she really was. He had changed from the disreputable denims and shirt, and was now wearing navy blue trousers and a light blue silk shirt that fitted tautly across his broad shoulders. He looked very lithe and attractive, emitting an aura of male dominance that made Katy feel protected and resentful at one and the same time.

He took her arm in a firm grasp. 'Drink?'

'Thank you,' she accepted gracefully.

He left her seated in one of the corner booths of the lounge-bar, going up to get their drinks. Katy couldn't see Gemma and Gerald anywhere in the room, so her gaze strayed back to Adam Wild as he chatted easily with the bartender. He was very self-assured, the lazy charm he displayed shielding a much more steely nature. Those warm blue eyes could harden with cruel anger, the relaxed body tense with fury. He had reached the top in a profession that was highly competitive, and he hadn't done it by sitting back and taking it easy.

'Thank you,' she accepted the Martini he put in front of her.

He relaxed back on the padded bench-seat next to her, his arm across the back of the seat and almost touching her. 'You're doing very well so far,' he said with amusement.

She gave him a sharp look. 'In what way?'

He shrugged, his expression amused. 'You haven't fallen over anything yet, not in my sight anyway, and the hotel still looks pretty much intact.'

Katy bristled angrily. 'Do you have to keep bringing up a few trifling mistakes I made on the plane? I can assure you I'm not usually so accident-prone.'

'I believe you,' he scorned.

'Tell me, Mr Wild,' she said sweetly, 'did you call me out of boredom or did you just lose your little black book for Canada?'

'Well, I certainly didn't lose my little black book,' he drawled infuriatingly.

'Thank you!'

He grinned. 'You asked for that one, Katy. Actually, the explanation is much more simple. I was neither bored nor bereft of my "little black book". I just happened to see your sister, put two and two together, and decided that there was no point in both of us being alone tonight.'

'I see.' Katy smoothed her dress down over her knees, then wished she hadn't as she realised she had drawn Adam's attention to the thigh-length slit up the side. Her cheeks warmed with colour as he made no effort to hide his interest.

'You have nice legs, too,' he remarked bluntly.

'Nice legs, shame about the face,' Katy taunted.

He took her remark seriously, seemingly giving each feature careful consideration. 'Nice face,' he corrected.

'But you've seen better,' she said dryly.

'Yes,' he agreed with cruel honesty.

She bent forward to pick up her drink. 'You—Oh, lord!' she broke off as the glass slipped out of her hand and the liquid flowed all over Adam Wild's trousers before the glass smashed on the floor at his feet. 'Oh no!' She looked at him in horror.

After an initial look of surprise a look of resignation passed over his features. 'I knew it was too good to last,' he groaned, mopping up the surplus Martini with a napkin.

'I couldn't help it,' Katy snapped. 'It just——'

His eyes went heavenwards. 'Where have I heard this before? Why is it it's never your fault? I didn't see anyone around when you dropped that little lot.'

Katy passed him another napkin. '*You* were.'

'So now it's my fault. Ugh!' he grimaced at the stickiness of his trousers. 'When you do something you really do it well!'

'Yes.' She stood up. 'I'll get someone to clean up the glass.'

'Don't bother.' He stood up too. 'I'll tell the barman. Then you can help me get cleaned up.'

'Oh, but——' He had already walked away, leaving her no choice but to wait for him outside.

He joined her within minutes. 'Let's go to your room,' he growled, the drink stained into the left side of his trousers.

Katy stopped in her tracks. '*My* room? But——'

'It has to be your room,' he said in exasperation. 'I don't happen to be staying here.'

'But——'

He pushed her into the lift. 'You seem to have got stuck on that word. Which floor?'

'Tenth. But—I mean,' she amended at his scathing look, 'if you aren't staying here why are you in the hotel?'

'Don't worry,' he scorned, 'I'm not following you. It just so happens that they serve a good steak here. The fact that you're staying in this hotel was merely a coincidence.'

'I'm sure it was.' She couldn't imagine him deliberately setting out to find any woman, they would always have to do the running where this man was concerned. 'I'm really sorry about your trousers.' Her look was rueful.

'So am I,' he said tersely. 'Unless you can get this Martini out you've just ruined a third of my wardrobe. I came away with two pairs of denims and these trousers,' he explained. 'And I didn't intend shopping for new clothes while I'm here.'

'It should sponge out.' She hoped! 'It was just an accident. I——'

'Accidents seem to follow you around.' They stepped out on to the tenth floor. 'Which room?'

Katy really had no choice. His trousers would have to be sponged before the liquid dried in and left a stain. 'This way.' She sounded disgruntled—and she was! To sponge his trousers he would have to take them off!

Katy blushed as Adam raised an eyebrow at the single bed in her room, keeping her expression enigmatic as she handed him her towelling robe. It would be a little short for him, but at least it would cover most of him—the most important part!

'The bathroom is through there,' she told him in a stilted voice.

While he was gone she straightened the rumpled bed, putting her discarded clothes back in her suitcase. She knew Adam Wild's sharp gaze hadn't missed the lacy bras and panties on top of her open suitcase, and she shut the lid with a bang.

She heard the bathroom door open behind her and knew he had taken his trousers off for her to clean. She held her breath and turned. The towelling robe managed to look masculine on him, barely reaching his thighs, and he had removed his shoes and socks too. Katy was glad about that, she might have laughed otherwise. There was something very funny about a man who had bare legs while still wearing his shoes and socks. At least, she thought there was.

Adam appeared unperturbed by his state of undress, totally sure of himself, and with good reason. His legs were long and muscular, with a fine sheen of dark hair on his tanned skin. Katy was mesmerised by him, and it was with great effort that she raised her darkened grey eyes to meet his curious stare. Her cheeks flamed as he seemed to guess her thoughts, a taunting smile playing about his lips.

'Give them to me,' she said sharply, holding out her hand for the trousers.

He held on to them. 'It says on the hotel card that they provide a cleaning service—a speedy cleaning service,' he added pointedly. 'So if you don't mind I won't leave my only decent pair of trousers to your tender mercies. Going on past record you'll probably rub a hole in them.' He picked up the telephone next to the bed.

Katy watched him do it. 'What are you doing?' she demanded to know.

He gave her a scathing glance. 'Calling for someone to collect my trousers,' he explained patiently.

'No!' Katy sprang forward and cut the connection off. 'You mustn't,' she said desperately. 'What will people think?'

Adam removed her hand from the telephone. 'I couldn't give a damn what people think. And I'll thank you not to touch this telephone again. Someone had just answered when you slammed your hand down on it. My trousers need cleaning, the hotel provide the service, so I intend letting them do it.'

'But you can't!' she insisted frantically. 'I—I only have a single room. What on earth will the management think if I send down a pair of men's trousers?'

'That you have a man in your room,' he drawled mockingly. 'What the hell does it matter what they think?' he added angrily.

'It matters to me. Oh, please, Adam,' she begged. 'I'll be careful with them—honestly I will.'

He began dialling. 'I'm sorry, Katy, but your careful isn't good enough.' He turned away to talk into the receiver.

Katy spun away from him. They were obviously an expensive pair of trousers, and as they were one of only three pairs he had with him he obviously wanted to take care of them, but it was very humiliating for her. She might only be staying in this hotel for one night, but she still didn't like people to think that she had been picked up by Adam Wild and had invited him back to her room. And that was how it was going to look, she knew that.

'Why do you only have a single room?'

She turned around at the sound of Adam talking to her, her eyes widening as she took in the fact that he was lying full length on her bed, his hands behind his head as he looked at her. The movement had hitched the towelling robe even farther up his legs, revealing that he wore black close-fitting underpants.

Katy had never been this close to a partially naked man before, and her heart skipped a few beats as she willed herself not to show how nervous she was. She knew by the amusement in his eyes that she hadn't succeeded, and his next remark confirmed it.

'I have more clothing on now than I would have on a beach,' he taunted her blushes.

'This isn't a beach,' she snapped. 'It's ten o'clock at

night, in my hotel room.'

He smiled. 'Does that make a difference?'

'Of course it does!'

'Why?'

'Don't be stupid!' Her eyes flashed.

'I think I get the picture,' he mocked. 'Because it's night-time and this is a hotel room I'm supposed to turn into some sort of sex maniac. You're the one that's being stupid, Katy,' he scorned. 'I don't have a specific time for making love. I get the urge in the morning, afternoon, *and* evening.'

'And I'm sure you get plenty of opportunities to satisfy this *urge*,' she said icily. 'I just——' she broke off as a knock sounded on the door. 'That will be the porter. Oh, dear, what shall I do?'

Adam shrugged. 'Well, I should open the door. Unless you would like me to?' He half rose from the bed.

'No! You stay where you are.'

'Gladly,' he drawled, dropping back on to the pillows.

Katy grabbed the trousers and made for the door. Her face was scarlet as she met the speculative look in the young boy's eyes.

She only opened the door far enough to hand the trousers out to him. 'I—Will it take long?' she asked nervously.

'About an hour, ma'am,' he said in a slow Canadian drawl.

An hour of Adam Wild lying half naked in her bedroom! 'No sooner than that?' she almost begged.

'Afraid not. You see——'

'Hurry up, darling,' Adam Wild called from inside the room. 'This bed is very lonely without you.'

The boy's speculation grew—and so did Katy's anger. 'Thank you,' she gave the boy a bright smile before turning furiously back into the room. 'How dare you!' she exploded. 'Why on earth did you do such a thing?'

He lay back, a lazy smile on his lips. 'He was bound to think that, I just didn't want him to be disappointed.'

Katy marched over to stand next to the bed, her expression one of indignation. 'You had no right—Oh!' she gasped as one of his hands snaked out and pulled her down beside him on the bed. 'Let me go!' She struggled against him.

'Don't be silly,' he murmured against her throat. 'You went to all this trouble, don't let's waste the opportunity now that we're here.'

'What trouble?' Katy fought against him, squirming as his lips probed the sensitive area beneath her earlobe. 'Stop that. Stop it!'

'Not on your life. I've had a lot of things tried on me, but no woman has ever gone to the lengths of tipping her drink down me to get my trousers off. You only had to ask, Katy, I would gladly have taken them off—for you.'

Anger burned deep within her. 'I didn't want your trousers off! And I certainly don't want you in my room. Now take your hands off me!'

'Just relax,' his breath was warm against her cheek, his mouth coming to the edge of her lips. 'Relax, Katy,' he groaned as her struggles began to ebb. 'Why fight what we both want?'

'But I don't. I don't!'

'Liar!'

She was a liar, she was even lying to herself. This man was an expert when it came to woman's sensuality, knowing exactly what areas of a woman's body to probe and caress. Katy had no defences against such expertise, trembling uncontrollably as his mouth finally claimed hers.

He was in no hurry to do more than kiss her, obviously thinking they had all night to progress. But his mouth on hers was enough to quell all the fight in her, taking her lips again and again as she lay beneath him. Katy hadn't known there were so many ways of kissing, with gentleness, with passion, and finally with thrusting savagery, his lips probing hers to deepen the caress. She had never known such intimacy, feeling as if he really did possess her in that moment, quivering helplessly against the hard length of his body.

'Aren't you going to touch me?' he whispered huskily.

'I—I've never——'

'Don't play the innocent with me, Katy Harris.' His voice hardened. 'That routine bores me. No girl, of eighteen or otherwise, is innocent nowadays. Women are born offering themselves.'

Katy gasped, 'That's a cynical attitude!'

'Learnt the hard way, little girl. Are you going to take this dress off or do you expect me to make love to you when you're fully clothed?' He pulled at the zip fastener at the back of her dress.

'No!' She stilled his movements, pulling away from him. 'I don't know what you think I am, Mr Wild, but I can assure you I don't hop into bed with a man I only met today.'

'Do I come back tomorrow?' He watched with narrowed eyes as she stood up to straighten her dress.

'I won't be here tomorrow,' she snapped.

'Neither will I—Thank God! You're a tease, do you know that? You've been giving me the green light ever since you got on the plane, and now I've decided to take you up on that offer you're playing hard to get.'

'Hard to get! Why, you——! You must be the most conceited man I've ever met! I've done nothing to encourage you, I even ripped up that card you gave me with your telephone number on.'

'Only so that I stayed interested. I bet you didn't rip up the second one?'

'Well . . . no. But——'

'I thought not. I've had every trick in the book tried on me, the "I'm not interested" routine is the most frequent.'

'And if a girl really isn't interested?' Katy demanded.

'That doesn't happen very often,' he said dryly.

'Well, it's happened this time,' she said with dislike. 'If and when I choose to sleep with a man I hope he doesn't have your conceit. How awful to make love to someone because you feel it's expected of you!'

Adam stiffened, his eyes hardening to blue slits. 'Is that why you think I did it?'

'Of course,' she scorned, moving to the other side of the room to look out over the lit-up Calgary. 'The irresistible Adam Wild has to keep up his reputation.'

'Reputation?'

'Oh yes. The newspapers are always reporting on your prowess. I've lost count of the number of women you've been seen escorting.'

He lounged comfortably on Katy's bed. 'If it's offered . . .'

'You take it,' she said disgustedly. 'Only this time it wasn't offered. And it never will be, not to you! You think you're so magnificent, don't you! Well, this is one time where you didn't strike lucky. You're the sort of man who most turns me off!'

'That wasn't the impression you gave a moment ago,' he drawled insultingly.

'How typical of you to bring up a thing like that!'

He smiled. 'You have to take what you can in today's world.'

'Well, I'm not for the taking! I wish your trousers would come back so that you can get out of here!'

'You can't wish it any more than I do,' he scowled.

'Then stop looking so damned comfortable. Why can't

you sit in one of the chairs instead of lounging about on my bed?'

'Because I *am* comfortable.' A knock sounded on the door. 'My trousers, I hope.'

It wasn't. Gemma stood outside the door. Katy kept the door half closed, her heart in her mouth. If Gemma should find Adam Wild in her bedroom . . .! She would never hear the end of it!

'Is there anything wrong?' she asked Gemma with a calm she was far from feeling.

'No, I just came to make sure you're all right. You aren't still sulking, are you?'

'I don't sulk,' Katy said stiffly. 'If you choose to sleep with Gerald then that's your business.'

'But you don't like it,' Gemma sighed.

'It isn't up to me to either like or dislike it, it's your decision.'

'You're such a prude.' She eyed Katy suspiciously. 'I thought you were going to have an early night?'

Katy blushed. 'I am. I'm just going to take a shower before going to bed. I——' Oh no! Behind Gemma she could see the porter stepping out of the lift with Adam Wild's newly cleaned trousers. She closed her eyes and waited for the inevitable.

'Here we are, ma'am,' the young boy grinned at her. 'I got them back just as soon as I could.'

'Thank you,' she said through stiff lips, handing him a tip from her purse.

'Thank *you*, ma'am.'

Gemma frowned, looking from Katy to the trousers and then back again. 'But what—— Who——'

'Mine, I believe,' drawled that deeply mocking voice.

Katy spun round to see Adam Wild standing beside her, the robe making the situation appear more intimate than it was. She almost groaned as Gemma's eyes widened with shock.

Adam took the trousers out of her hand. 'Good evening, Miss Harris,' he greeted Gemma. 'I hope you'll excuse me while I get dressed?'

'Katy!' Gemma sounded scandalised, watching as Adam walked into the bathroom. She turned blazing eyes on Katy. 'And you dared to disapprove of me! My God,' she gave a bitter laugh, 'you're even worse than me. You only met the man today, and already you've been to bed with him. Well, in future don't you dare to preach to me,' she ended fiercely. 'Goodnight!'

Katy watched her sister leave, turning angrily to tackle Adam Wild.

CHAPTER THREE

'You did that on purpose!' she attacked him as soon as he came out into the main room.

He was looking his calm, assured self, handing her the towelling robe. 'Of course I did. Your sister was right about you, you are a prude.'

'I am not!'

'Yes, you are.' He finished tucking his shirt into the low waistband of his trousers, the movement straining the pale blue shirt across his taut muscular stomach and wide powerful shoulders. 'So that's why you have a single room. At least your sister isn't ashamed to let people know she's sleeping with her boy-friend.'

'*You* don't happen to be my boy-friend. I doubt you've ever been any woman's *boy-friend*.'

'How right you are! I've never met a woman yet who could be entertaining out of bed as well as in it.'

Her eyes blazed, green sparks visible among the grey. 'I suppose that's where you think we belong, between the sheets.'

'Or on them,' Adam taunted. 'I'm not that fussy where it happens. A change of locality can make it more interesting.'

'I'm sure you've tried it at every locality and in every situation imaginable,' Katy said insultingly.

He shrugged. 'You could be right. Have a nice holiday,' came his parting taunt.

Nice holiday! How could she, when her own sister thought her little more than a tramp, capable of going to bed with a man just because he was rich and famous?

She knew by the open mockery on Gerald's face the

47

next day that Gemma had told him all about finding Adam Wild in her room. By the time they had picked up the camper and were setting out for Banff Katy had had enough of his knowing looks.

'Why don't you just come out with it?' she snapped angrily. 'Just say it and get it over with!'

He gave her a look of exaggerated innocence. 'Why, what do you mean, Katy?'

'It's disgusting!' Gemma suddenly burst out, giving her a scathing look. 'At least Gerald and I are engaged!'

'And I suppose that excuses your behaviour?'

'It explains it.' Gemma refused to be angered. 'Just because Adam Wild expressed an interest in you, you didn't have to go to bed with him! No wonder you hung about the airport with him long after Gerald and I had passed through!'

'After you'd left me, you mean.'

'Huh! And you do realise that the offer to photograph you no longer stands, not now he's seen all of you?'

'He hasn't!' But it was true, once he had seen all of her body he would know that she wasn't photographable, not with her scars.

'He's had what he wants from you.' Gemma spoke dismissively.

Gerald's gaze ran over Katy speculatively. 'You really are a dark horse. I would never have believed it of you if Gemma hadn't seen you with her own eyes.'

'I've already explained to Gemma what she saw!' Katy almost exploded with the frustration of this situation.

'A likely story.' Again Gemma dismissed what even Katy realised was a feeble story—even if it was true. 'You could have warned me he was in your room. I could have died of embarrassment when he appeared at the doorway wearing *your* towelling robe.'

Katy sighed. 'I've told you——'

'Save your breath,' her sister said crossly. 'And I don't want a repeat of this behaviour while we're here. I don't intend getting you out of every tricky situation you stupidly get yourself into. After all, you are my kid sister, Katy, and Mum and Dad would blow their top if they found out about last night.'

'Do you intend telling them?'

'Not if you don't tell them about Gerald and me.'

Katy gasped, 'That's blackmail!'

Gemma smiled. 'Fair's fair.'

'I didn't intend telling Mum and Dad about you. But you can tell them what you please about me, it wouldn't be true anyway.' Katy held her head proudly erect.

'So you say,' Gerald grinned. 'That man's reputation is well known. I shouldn't think there's one model he's photographed who hasn't got into bed with him afterwards. And that amounts to hundreds.'

Katy could believe it, in fact Adam Wild had more or less admitted it. She went back to sitting in the dinette part of the camper, Gerald in the driving seat and Gemma in the sext next to him. Not that Katy minded, being free to admire what was turning out to be beautiful scenery.

The flatness of Calgary had now given way to first what looked like small hills and then towering mountains. Pine trees reached almost to the edge of the road, going far up into the mountains, stopping at what Adam Wild had told her was the timberline. Wisps of downy clouds nestled on the top of the mountains, looking like soft white candyfloss.

Katy was enthralled. This was the Canada she had come to see, the highway through the Canadian Rockies, one of the most scenic routes in the country. And then came the snow on the mountain peaks, snow that remained on the mountains all year round because the temperature was so cold up there it wasn't able to melt.

The drive to Banff seemed to take no time at all, so engrossed was Katy in her surroundings, each mile seeming more beautiful than the last. Therefore it came as something of a surprise to her when shortly after five o'clock they drove into the town of Banff. Not that it was like any English town she had ever seen; the houses seemed to have been built in a clearing of the towering green pine trees, and the woodlands and mountains dominated everything in their path.

The main street seemed to be mainly restaurants and gift shops, Katy noted as they slowly drove through, although she did see a couple of museums she thought would bear closer inspection, and people were standing to be photographed beside the totem pole erected outside one of them.

'I'm not sure we should camp out,' Gemma remarked nervously. 'They had a bear attack at one of the campsites in the park last week. Some poor man was badly mauled.'

'Where did you hear that?' Gerald scorned.

'I overheard someone at the hotel.'

'They were probably exaggerating. I doubt we'll even see a bear, let alone get attacked by one.'

'But they said——'

'Forget it, Gemma,' he dismissed. 'Bear attacks aren't exactly common over here.'

'I know. It's just that it's made me feel nervous. There's supposed to be bears all over these National Parks—wild bears.'

Gerald spluttered with laughter. 'Well, of course they're wild, that's the whole idea of these parks, to give the animals miles and miles of freedom.'

'I'm just not sure I want to camp out,' Gemma insisted.

'Why didn't you mention this earlier,' he said crossly, 'before we picked up the camper? You can't expect us to book into a motel when we have our accommodation right here. I'm certainly not going to.'

Neither was Katy. Part of the reason she had agreed to come on this holiday was because they would be able to camp out and provide their own meals when they wanted them. Staying in a cosy motel wasn't part of her plan.

'I suppose not,' Gemma agreed reluctantly. 'Where shall we camp, then?'

'Well, it has to be one of the official sites, it's against the law to camp anywhere else,' Gerald informed them knowledgeably. 'There's one up in the mountains here somewhere, I fancy that one.'

It wasn't difficult to find and they were soon paying their nominal fee at the gate, a fee that helped keep the parks clean and in their natural state of beauty.

Gemma was sorting through the information sheets they had been handed at the gate. 'Look at this,' she held up one of the sheets of paper. 'It's a warning about the bears.'

'Just a precaution,' Gerald soothed, as he drove down to their site. 'We aren't allowed to light fires up here,' he said regretfully. 'Pity, I fancied a barbecue.'

'I'm certainly not going to cook outside if there are bears about!' Gemma seemed genuinely frightened.

Katy took the typewritten sheet from her. 'We'll be perfectly all right if we follow the advice on here. Most of it's just common sense anyway.'

Gemma grimaced. 'It says on there that you aren't to feed the bears. As if I would!'

Her fiancé laughed. 'Never mind, darling. Banff has one advantage, a swimming pool with water from the hot springs.' He smiled at her. 'You'll like that, hmm?'

'Yes.' Some of her nervousness seemed to recede. 'I brought my bikini with me, but the rivers and lakes look too cold to swim in.'

'We can go on to Radium Hot Springs tomorrow if you like, they have a pool there too.'

Katy grimaced behind them. She hadn't expected to go from one swimming spot to another, especially as she herself rarely swam, being too conscious of the scars she had acquired on her back as a child. If they had wanted to swim then perhaps they should have gone to one of the coastal resorts. She couldn't understand why they had come on this sort of holiday in the first place, not when Gemma liked her creature comforts so much. And Gemma had always been nervous of animals, even the sort behind bars in a zoo. Personally Katy abhorred zoos and all that they stood for, and she admired the Canadians for keeping these huge parks, hundreds of square miles of them, where the wildlife could live as it was meant to, completely free and away from human beings if they chose to.

They were certainly nothing like the wildlife parks in England, where animals were still kept behind wire fences, in compounds that weren't big enough to be one animal's territory, let alone the dozen or so it usually contained. Here the animals *were* free, the people were the intruders, and that was the way it should be.

'I think I'll go up in the gondola lift while you two swim,' she said now. 'Gemma always gets sick on those sort of things.'

'They're too much like a combination of the Big Wheel and the Big Dipper,' her sister shuddered.

'Now that we have a site we might as well go into town and grab a meal,' Gerald suggested. 'Neither of you is that great a cook, so we might as well eat out whenever we can.'

'Thanks!' Katy grimaced. 'I'm not sure I mind your derogatory remarks about my cooking, but I think Gemma might.'

He grinned. 'I'm not marrying her for her cooking ability.'

His fiancée giggled, 'I have other talents.'

Katy turned away. She was absolutely dreading tonight. The camper was a large one, with a separate room at the back containing bunk-beds, but it certainly didn't allow for the privacy of a couple who wanted to do more than sleep. She had decided to sleep on the lower bunk-bed while Gemma and Gerald would sleep in the double bed over the driving area; that way she would be as far away from them as she could be. Even so, she wasn't looking forward to it.

They found a restaurant in town with a vacant booth, although all the eating places seemed to be very busy, this being one of the few towns among the Canadian Rockies, and so very popular with the tourists, who hiked and drove through here most of the year.

Once again Katy felt warmed by the friendliness of the people, finding them eager to know whereabouts in England they came from. They always told them near London, although they were in fact about forty miles away. Katy's father was a doctor in a sleepy little Hampshire village. But everyone had heard of London, England, whereas not too many people seemed to have heard of Hampshire, England.

None of the meals seemed to come small over here, as Katy was learning to her cost. If she weren't careful she would put on pounds during the next two weeks. As it was she could only manage to eat half the steak on her plate, although Gerald seemed to have no trouble eating all of his, and a dessert. Gemma was defeated early, like Katy, although she watched fondly as Gerald ate his apple pie.

Katy found her sister's open adoration for this man pretty sickening, and she was glad when they all left the restaurant. It was a sure fact *she* was never going to fall for a man as completely as that. No man was going to make her his slave, in any way.

Her thoughts came back to Adam Wild. Really their attitudes weren't so unalike; he wanted to remain free of emotional entanglements too. But they did differ. He wasn't averse to making women fall for him, he just had no intention of reciprocating the feeling, whereas Katy wanted her marriage to be a partnership, an equal amount of giving and taking on both sides. Adam Wild was a man who took everything offered to him, accepted it all as his due, and maybe in a way it was. Any girl who fell for him deserved what she got.

When Gemma suggested a game of cards later that evening Katy readily agreed, although she made her excuses at an early hour so that she might endeavour to be asleep before the other two retired for the night. She did fall asleep quite early, but her sister's giggling soon woke her up, and her face burnt with embarrassment as she realised what must be going on out there. When she couldn't stand their heated murmurings any longer she pulled the pillow over her head, praying for sleep. It finally came to her, but not until the early hours of the morning.

She was hollow-eyed and pale the next morning, whereas Gemma looked glowingly beautiful. Maybe love affected one like that. Gerald seemed to think so, for Katy's own appearance was soon noticed by him.

'You'll have to get yourself a man,' he taunted her. 'Missing Adam Wild, are you?'

'No, I'm not!'

'You look like a frustrated old maid,' he told her.

'At eighteen?' she scorned.

'At any age when you know someone else is getting what you aren't.'

Katy turned away, her face fiery red. 'You're crude!'

'I know,' he grinned leeringly. 'But Gemma doesn't mind.'

Katy's nose wrinkled with distaste. 'I can't stand crudeness. Now are we going into town or not?'

'We are. Gem and I have been looking forward to our swim. Sure you don't want to come with us?'

'Sure.' Even more sure today. She just wanted to get away from them as soon as possible.

The pool and the lift up Sulphur Mountain were more or less next to each other, so they parted company in the car park, arranging to meet up later. Minutes later Katy felt glad she had gone alone. She couldn't have borne Gemma's feelings of sickness as the chairlift rocked out on to its ascent. The gondola could hold four people, but at the moment this one only contained her. Once started on its climb it went quite smoothly, giving Katy the chance to take some photographs on the way up. It started to get quite breezy towards the top and was quite cold when she stepped out on to the summit.

The view was spectacular, and Katy spent half an hour or more taking photographs. Scenes like this had to be seen to be believed, and her mother and father would enjoy looking at her snapshots.

'Your angle's all wrong,' drawled a deeply familiar voice. 'From this angle you're going to get more of the chairlift structure than the actual chairs coming up the mountain.'

Katy spun round to face her tormentor. 'Don't you have something better to do than be sarcastic to me, Mr Wild?'

He shrugged. 'I wasn't being sarcastic, just offering sound advice. But if you don't want it . . .' He turned away.

What an idiot she was—after all, he was the professional photographer. She caught up with him outside the tea-house. 'I'm sorry.' He didn't seem to have heard her, so she touched his arm. 'Hey, Adam, I'm sorry. I—I didn't mean to be rude.'

He shrugged her hand off; he was dressed as casually as when they had first met, although the denims and matching shirt looked newly laundered. 'Maybe I deserved it— we didn't part the best of friends.'

'No, we didn't,' she agreed with remembered anger. 'I haven't forgiven you for that yet. Gemma and Gerald haven't let me forget it.'

'I'll bet,' he grinned. 'Maybe they just needed reminding that you're a desirable young woman.'

'I don't think they ever knew it in the first place,' she grimaced.

'A pity. Fancy a coffee?' he indicated the building behind them.

'I thought it was a teahouse?' Katy teased.

He gave her a scathing look. 'They serve coffee too.'

'Good,' she smiled at him for the first time. 'I'm not all that keen on tea.'

'God, you must be lonely!'

'I must?' She followed him in and sat down at one of the tables while he went up to get their coffee. 'Why must I?' she resumed their conversation as he sat down opposite her.

'You're actually being pleasant to me.'

Katy looked down at her cup. 'I'm sorry—about before.' She added sugar to her coffee and kept stirring and stirring.

Adam's hand came out to stop her, keeping hold of it to caress her palm with his thumb. 'Where are your sister and her loving fiancé?'

His description brought embarrassing memories to mind, and she blushed a fiery red. 'They've gone swimming,' she mumbled.

'But not you?'

'Not me.' His gaze probed and she turned away.

'Didn't you realise what it would be like when you agreed to come here?' He sounded impatient.

'Of course I didn't,' her eyes flashed, 'or I wouldn't be here.'

He raised his eyebrows, shaking his head. 'Poor innocent Katy!'

'Not so innocent!' she snapped. 'You still have hold of my hand,' she said pointedly.

'So I do.' He made no effort to relinquish it. 'Would you rather come with me?' he asked softly.

Her eyes widened. 'I beg your pardon?'

Adam gave a half smile. 'You heard me. You may find it less embarrassing travelling with me. And I'm sure your sister and her Romeo would have no objections.'

'Maybe not, but I would. I know Gerald told me to find myself a man, but even he didn't mean someone like you.'

His deep blue eyes narrowed in anger. 'Like me?' His voice was dangerously soft.

'You know what I mean,' she avoided looking at him.

'I think I do. I was just offering you a way out, Katy,' he grated. 'By the look of you you need it.'

She put up a selfconscious hand to her pale cheeks. 'I just didn't sleep well.'

'I can imagine why.' His mouth twisted.

'You're as crude as he is!' she snapped.

'He?'

'Gerald!' she said disgustedly, finally managing to pull her hand away from him, telling herself that she didn't really feel that tingling sensation up her arm. 'He seems to think I'm frustrated,' she added crossly.

'And are you?'

'No, I'm not!'

'Good, then you won't mind listening to them for the

next two weeks.' He so obviously regretted his offer of a few minutes ago. 'Are you ready to leave?' he stood up.

'Oh—oh yes.' Katy gulped down the last of her coffee, not eager to be on her own again. She might find his company disturbing, but it was better than being alone. She followed him out into the brisk breeze. 'How did you get here?' she asked conversationally.

Adam gave her a pitying look. 'The same way you did, in the chair-lift. I'm not one of your physical fitness freaks. I would have collapsed halfway if I'd walked up.'

'I would have thought with all the exercise you get you would be very fit,' she taunted.

'That sort of exercise just makes me fit for exercise of the same sort,' he rasped. 'As you're going to find out if you don't behave yourself.'

Katy blushed. 'That wasn't what I meant anyway. I meant how did you get to Banff?'

Adam took her arm and led her to the left of the tea-house. 'Jud lent me his transport while he's out of town.'

He was leading her down a rough track and Katy looked at him enquiringly. 'Where are you taking me?'

He gave a leering smile, towering over her. 'I'm taking you off to ravish you among the pine trees. Not really,' he openly laughed at her nervous expression. 'You do won-ders for my ego, Katy. I get quite a kick out of being thought a sex maniac.'

'Then where are we going?' she asked irritably, ignoring his taunting.

'Down,' he continued walking.

Katy gaped at him. 'Down . . .?'

'That's right.'

She looked down to the bottom of the mountain. It looked miles. 'All the way down there?' she gulped.

'All the way,' Adam confirmed. 'Something I'll bet you've never done before.'

Colour stained her cheeks; his double meaning was not lost on her. 'I'm not wearing the right shoes for walking,' she complained. 'Besides, it's too far.'

'Only three miles—I checked.'

'Three——! I'm not walking three miles down this muddy trail!' She came to an abrupt halt.

'Oh yes, you are,' he insisted, pulling her along behind him. 'It will walk off your frustration.'

'I am not frustrated!'

'Like me to prove otherwise?' He quirked an eyebrow.

'I might,' she met his challenge, tired of his taunts.

Adam looked down at her for long silent minutes. 'You don't really mean that.'

'Try me.'

He eyed the pine trees on the edge of the narrow pathway. 'In there?'

'No! Oh, forget it. I just thought——'

'You just thought you should have taken advantage of the offer the first time it was going! That's okay, Katy, the offer's still there.' Before she could offer any resistance he had pulled her into his arms and ground his mouth savagely down on hers. When he raised his head there was still anger in his eyes. 'How was that?' he rasped harshly.

Katy put up a hand to her sore mouth, aware that it had been his resentment over the things she had said to him that had caused this onslaught. He wasn't a man she should have angered—and especially not part way down a mountain where there was no one to help her if he should—if he should——

'Don't worry,' he scorned, 'I'm not going to rape you. But stick to your own league in future, little girl.' He still held her curved against the hard contours of his body. 'I could eat you up and not even notice.'

'Could you really?' she tilted her head back bravely.

'I'd like to see you try!'

Smiling, he put her away from him, a smile that held no humour. 'Don't tempt me.'

'Excuse me . . .?'

They turned to see a middle-aged couple in hiking gear standing a few feet away from them, unable to get past because they were blocking the pathway.

'Certainly.' Adam pulled Katy to one side. 'Sorry about that. Just keeping her in line,' he grinned.

'I'll have to try that,' the husband smiled, moving past them.

The plump wife eyed Adam. 'I don't think it would be the same coming from you, dear,' and she turned and walked on.

Katy spluttered with laughter once the other couple were safely out of earshot. 'Poor man,' she sympathised, smiling broadly.

Adam watched her warily, obviously surprised at her laughter. 'What's so funny?' he frowned.

'I couldn't help thinking the same as that woman. I'd much rather be kissed by you than her husband, too,' she admitted.

The tension seemed to leave his body. 'I shouldn't let you anger me. Come on,' he put his arm about her shoulders, 'it should only take us a couple of hours to get to the bottom.'

'Oh no!' Katy protested. 'Gemma and Gerald will be waiting for me.'

'Then they'll just have to wait.'

'Yes, but——'

'Walk, Katy.'

They talked little on the way down, as the narrowness of the trail did not allow them to walk side by side in comfort. Katy was beginning to feel haunted by this man. Wherever she went he seemed to be there, not that he seemed any happier to see her than she was him.

Why had he asked her to go with him? Maybe he was bored with his own company already; he probably had a woman in his bed every night when he was at home. Much as she wanted to get away from Gemma and Gerald's *loving* company she couldn't go with Adam Wild. She wasn't going to become his plaything.

They reached the car park exactly one hour and forty-five minutes later, Katy completely out of breath, with flushed cheeks and fever-bright eyes, and Adam Wild looking as if he had been for an afternoon stroll. So much for him being out of condition.

As he had been walking in front of her most of the time she had had ample opportunity to look at him without fear of his mocking her. He was lean and fit, firmly muscled, which didn't point to him leading the disreputable life she had accused him of. He might be cynical about women but that didn't mean he was dissipated. In fact, she was now sure he wasn't. He was just a very attractive man who got sick and tired of women throwing themselves at him, especially when he suspected their motives. If only he would realise he was attractive enough to have those women chase him even without the added bonus of him possibly being able to make them famous through his expert camerawork.

Katy brought herself up with a start. This wouldn't do, she couldn't become attracted to him. He was too old for her, for one thing, even older than his thirty-six years in experience, and besides, he had no real use for women, no respect for them. They were just toys to him, and when he became bored with a certain toy he just replaced it.

'Where on earth have you been?' Gemma appeared at her side, a furiously angry Gemma, her eyes sparkling with temper. 'We've been waiting ages for you. You're over an hour late,' she accused.

Katy looked guiltily down at her mud-spattered shoes. 'Yes, well—— You see——'

'It was my fault, I'm afraid,' Adam intervened smoothly. 'I delayed her.'

Gemma's eyes widened with recognition and she looked suspiciously at Katy. 'You didn't tell us you were meeting Mr Wild,' she said tightly.

'Oh, but I——'

'Don't bother to explain,' her sister sighed, obviously misunderstanding the reason for Katy's flushed and dishevelled appearance. 'We'll be waiting for you over there.' She marched off to join Gerald, who was already seated in the camper.

'Whoops!' Adam smiled, looking down at Katy's woebegone face. 'Hey, cheer up, it was only an hour.'

'You don't understand,' she mumbled.

'Sure I do. They'll make your life a misery from now on.' He gently lifted her head by placing a finger under her chin. 'Come with me, Katy,' he repeated his offer of earlier. 'I'm sure you would—enjoy yourself more with me.'

She flushed. 'I'm sure I would,' she swung away from him. 'I have to go now. I—— Thank you for today.'

He shrugged and stepped back. 'My pleasure,' he drawled dryly. 'It would be too much of a coincidence for us to meet again, so don't forget to call me when you get back to London. Jud agreed with me about your body.'

Katy gasped. 'You *told* him? Oh God,' she groaned, 'how embarrassing!'

'It would only be that if you saw him again, and I doubt there's any likelihood of that.'

'Thank God!' Her eyes glittered palely grey. 'You really are outrageous. Don't you ever see women as anything other than bodies?'

His look was cold. 'They have little else to recommend them.'

'Thanks very much!' She spun on her heel and walked away. Hateful, hateful man! She had thought their truce too good to last.

Gemma and Gerald's displeasure could be felt when she got into the camper, although they maintained a stony silence until they got back to the campsite, when Gemma turned on her angrily. 'The next time you arrange to meet that man you might have the decency to tell us. We checked with the people at the chair-lift that you'd gone up the mountain, but they didn't remember you coming down again. We were just about to come up there ourselves.'

'We walked down,' Katy mumbled, knowing that she deserved their anger. She would have been furious if they had kept her waiting. 'But I didn't arrange to meet him,' she defended. 'It was purely accidental.'

Gemma scoffed her disbelief of that and Katy didn't argue with her. After that evening in her hotel room the evidence was too damning. Instead she changed the subject. 'Are you staying here again tonight?'

'We might as well,' came Gerald's grumbling reply. 'It's too late to get down to Radium Hot Springs today.'

Her fault. 'Did you enjoy your swim?' she tried again.

'It was lovely.' Gemma thawed a little. 'You'll have to try it tomorrow.'

'Maybe.' Katy heaved an inward sigh of relief. The last thing she wanted to do in the confined space of the camper was to fall out with her sister and Gerald. Besides, she had been in the wrong.

She played it safe that night, opting to go for a walk when Gemma and Gerald decided to go to bed. Perhaps they would be asleep by the time she got back. She walked down the road and into the wood, finding the silence eerie this time of night. But the smell of the pines was intoxicating, and she watched in fascination as a couple of deer fed in a clearing. She forgot the time, forgot everything but the complete naturalness of the animals as they played, unaware of her presence there.

It was very late when she went back, and she had trouble finding the camper at first. It was in darkness and she let herself in quietly, congratulating herself on her evasive tactics. She didn't feel in quite such a good humour when she saw her sleeping bag neatly tied up and stacked in the corner of her bunk, her nightgown missing completely. Gerald's idea of a joke, no doubt. Well, she didn't think it at all funny as she stumbled about in the darkness. It would serve them right if she went out there and gave them a piece of her mind!

She was so angry that she had trouble falling asleep, her resentment towards them immense, so that it was almost light before she finally fell asleep. She was woken up by the sound of the engine starting up, and she snuggled down into her sleeping bag before falling asleep again. If they couldn't be bothered to give her breakfast then she couldn't be bothered to get out of bed.

It was almost lunchtime when she woke up again, Gerald having apparently found somewhere for them to eat. She sat up, yawning, the rumblings of her stomach telling her she was ready for a meal. At least Gerald seemed to be in a good humour this morning, whistling to himself, and was that coffee she smelt? She hoped so.

She brightened as a knock came on the door. 'Come in!' She hastily straightened the sleeping bag to cover her nakedness.

'Here,' a coffee cup appeared in front of her. 'And make the most of it—after today I'll expect you to get *me* coffee in bed.'

All colour had drained from Katy's face, and she looked up into the mockingly sensual face of Adam Wild.

CHAPTER FOUR

IT couldn't be, not *Adam Wild*! But it was, and looking just as handsome as usual, a dark blue shirt tucked into the low waistband of his tight-fitting denims.

The cup in Katy's hand shook so much that the coffee spilt over into the saucer. 'What are you doing here?' she collected her scattered wits enough to ask.

He shrugged, making no effort to hide his interest in her nakedness inside the sleeping bag. 'I'm living here— for the moment.'

'Here?' she repeated dazedly. 'But Gemma and Gerald——'

'Are probably still in Banff,' he finished in a bored voice. 'Come on, lazybones, it's time for lunch. Or do you want me to eat you instead?' His deep blue eyes caressed her.

'Certainly not!' Katy clutched the cover to her. 'How can Gemma and Gerald still be in Banff? If they were I would still be with them. Why can't you leave me alone, stop following me!'

'*I'm* following you? My dear Katy, you've done nothing but make a nuisance of yourself since we first met. And it would seem,' anger entered his voice, 'that once again you've mucked things up—for want of a better word,' he added dryly. 'Just where the hell do you think you are?'

'Radium Hot Springs?' she suggested hopefully.

Adam sighed impatiently, running a hand absently through the thick darkness of his over-long hair. 'That wasn't what I meant. Where do you think you are at this precise moment?'

'In bed, in the camper we hired,' she frowned her puzzlement.

'Half right. Oh God, what a bloody stupid female you are!' he raised his eyes heavenwards. 'You are in bed, that part is right, but this happens to be my camper—or at least Jud's, which he's lent me for the duration of my stay here.'

Grey eyes opened wide with fear. 'You—your camper? But I—it can't be,' she protested weakly.

'But it is,' he mocked tersely. 'Get out of bed and see for yourself. You'll find a lot of personal changes in the main part of the vehicle, enough to convince you I haven't stolen your sister's camper and dumped them in some deserted wood.'

Colour flooded her pale cheeks. 'I—I can't get out of bed, not until you leave. I—I don't have any clothes on.'

'That doesn't bother me, sweetie,' he smiled, eyeing her expectantly.

'Well, it bothers me! I'd like some privacy while I dress, if you don't mind—even if you *do* mind,' she added before he could taunt her again.

'Okay,' he gave a careless shrug, as if one more female body was no novelty to him. 'But don't be long.'

Katy must have set the record for getting dressed, terrified he would open the door before she had her clothes on. This *couldn't* be Jud Turner's camper, it just couldn't be! And yet she had a dreadful feeling that it was, and that the rolled-up sleeping bag and absent nightgown were not due to a practical joke at all.

When she stepped out into the main living area it was to find it as Adam Wild had said she would, the kitchen area completely different, and the dinette a permanent fixture instead of the conversion to a double bed that they had. Also there were posters stuck on every available piece of wall, some of them showing nude women.

Katy sank down on to the luxury leather sofa, another extra, feeling as if her legs would no longer support her. 'Oh God,' she groaned. 'This really is Jud Turner's camper.'

'Right down to the nudes,' Adam mocked, handing her the coffee she hadn't drunk earlier. 'I've heated it up for you.'

She took a sip, a fiery liquid passing down her throat and burning her as it went. 'My God,' she choked, 'what did you put in it?' She screwed up her face.

'Whisky,' he grinned. 'I told you I'd heated it up. I thought you might need the whisky to help you over your shock.'

Katy gave him a look of intense dislike, and put the coffee cup down on the side. 'I'm not in shock. Now it seems there's been some sort of mistake——'

'And you made it!'

She glared at him. 'So it would appear. Just where are we?'

'At a restaurant just after the turn-off for Red Deer. I stopped for petrol and thought we could eat at the same time.'

'Red Deer?' she echoed dully. 'But that's——'

'In the opposite direction to Radium Hot Springs,' he finished for her.

'Oh no!' again she groaned. Suddenly she frowned. 'You said you thought *we* could eat—did you know I was here all the time?'

'Sure,' he nodded.

'How did you know?'

'I heard you crashing about last night as you made yourself comfortable in the bedroom. I sleep in the double bed over the driving area, I'm used to more room than there is in a bunk bed.'

'You *heard* me? And yet you said nothing?' she said shrilly.

'It's a woman's prerogative to change her mind.'

'About what did I change my mind?'

He sighed. 'About making the rest of the trip with me.'

Katy blushed, her eyes flaring with anger. 'I took a walk,' she told him resentfully. 'I got slightly lost and must have got into the wrong camper, I did not change my mind about coming with you.'

'You *took a walk*?' he exploded, every muscle tensed with anger. 'Where?' he demanded to know.

Her eyes were wide. 'Just in the woods a little way. I saw some deer and——'

'You wandered off into the forest?' There could be no doubt about his anger now, his face harsh. 'You just walked in there like you were taking a Sunday afternoon stroll in a park in England?'

'I was perfectly safe.'

'Safe?' he derided tautly. '*Safe!*' His fingers dug into her arms as he pulled her roughly to her feet. 'You thought yourself safe out there with wild bears roaming about! Maybe you were right, you would certainly be safer with one of them at this moment than you are with me. Of all the stupid, idiotic—— My God, Katy!' he groaned before his mouth ground down on hers in a kiss that was meant to cause pain—and did.

Katy had gone numb at his mention of the bears, offering no resistance as his mouth plundered hers, his arms crushing her to the hardness of his body. One hand moved up to grasp a handful of her hair, holding her head immobile as he continued to punish her with the cruelty of his mouth, the fingers of his other hand still pressed painfully into her arm.

His eyes were glittering, his breathing laboured when he at least released her. He put her away from him with a disgusted look. 'Did you think yourself safe, or did you just think all those warnings about bears were a joke?' he snapped.

She felt dazed, and not just by the mention of the bears. 'I—We heard about the attack, of course, but——'

'You just dismissed it,' Adam flared. 'You don't just dismiss the bears in these parks, they're the real thing. And you keep the hell out of their way!'

'But the attack wasn't in Banff, it was at Lake Louise, and——'

'And you think that's the only bear in the park?' He shook his head disgustedly. 'There are hundreds of them here, and a tasty little morsel like you might make a nice variation on their diet. The last person who went for a little stroll at night had his leg ripped off for his trouble.' His gaze passed down the length of her slender legs clearly outlined in her denims. 'You wouldn't look so good with only one leg,' he said cruelly.

Katy was white with reaction now. She had been out for over an hour last night, an hour when a bear could have—Oh God, she felt sick!

'Not in here,' Adam said unsympathetically. 'Use the bathroom if you have to.'

She swallowed hard, fighting down the nausea. 'I'm all right now,' she said weakly.

'Then you damn well ought not to be! Haven't you read the leaflets? No one, but no one, tempts fate in that way.'

'All right!' She pushed her tangled hair out of her face, wanting to brush it, but was almost frightened to move with Adam in this mood. 'So I shouldn't have gone for that walk, I think you've made your point.'

'I'd better have,' he threatened darkly. 'What on earth were you doing walking that time of night? Why—Ah, I see it all now,' he said knowingly. 'You wanted to get away from the nocturnal murmurings of your sister and her boy-friend.'

Colour flooded her cheeks. 'I just wanted some air,' she defended. 'I can't understand how I got back in the wrong camper.'

'Quite easily, I should imagine. A lot of them look alike. This is pretty standard—from the outside. I don't suppose you noticed the different interior in the dark.'

She shivered. 'I could have got in with anyone!'

'I doubt it,' Adam said dryly. 'Not the amount of noise you made. I only let you stay because I thought you wanted to be here.'

'And now you know I don't?' At last she dared to get her brush out of her handbag and put some order to her tangled tresses. At least she had her handbag with her, had her money and some basic cosmetics—not that she had thought to use any of the latter, she had been in too much of a hurry. She doubted Adam Wild was accustomed to seeing women who weren't perfectly made up and groomed. His women were always models, very occasionally actresses, and she couldn't see any of them being caught without their full make up.

Adam shrugged. 'We'll have to let the authorities know you're all right. You do realise,' his voice was harsh, 'that once you were known to be missing there would be a search set up for you?'

'Oh no!'

'Oh yes. You were one thoughtless female, Katy Harris. I've known some pretty stupid females in my time, but I think you take first prize.' He pulled on a worn black leather jacket.

'Where are you going?' She ignored his insults, knowing she deserved them. It had been a stupid thing to do.

'To use the telephone. I haven't heard anything on the radio about a missing girl, but then I may have missed it.

We'll call them and let them know you aren't missing at all.'

Once outside they found all of the four public telephones in use. 'Go and wait for me inside,' Adam ordered as a cold wind blew down on them. 'I shouldn't be long,' he added as one of the telephones became vacant.

'But——'

'Go inside, Katy.' His expression told her that he had come to the end of his patience with her stupidity.

She went, mainly because she didn't want to anger him any more. There were a couple of artists at work around the front of the wooden building, and Katy could sympathise with their frozen-looking hands. The weather was much cooler here, the snow heavier on the surrounding mountains. It looked as if winter were coming early to this beautiful part of Canada.

She paid for the two coffees and sat down to wait for Adam. If there really had been a search going on for her she was going to be decidedly unpopular, and not just with Gemma and Gerald!

Adam looked infinitely more relaxed when he entered the cafeteria, his blue eyes searching the room until he saw her sitting meekly in a corner. Several female heads turned to watch him as he walked over to Katy, and she wasn't surprised by their interest. He was easily the best looking man in the room, moving with a lazy indolence she was finding was totally deceptive. He was an astute, clever man, and he had little patience with fools.

'Thanks.' He sipped the coffee she had got him, adding no sweetening. 'Well, you're in the clear as far as a search goes.'

Relief flooded over her. 'You mean they didn't make one?'

He shook his head. 'They didn't have time.'

Katy frowned her bewilderment. 'Didn't have time . . .?'

'I don't mean they were too busy,' Adam said impatiently. 'I meant that they didn't have time between you being reported missing and my reporting you found again.'

'But I've been gone for hours!'

'Apparently your sister and Romeo didn't know that. When you didn't answer their knock this morning they thought you were sulking and left you to it. Their words, not mine,' he drawled.

Her eyes widened. 'You spoke to them?'

'To Gemma,' he confirmed.

'She was there?'

'Mm. And she isn't feeling very sisterly towards you at the moment.'

'But where are they?'

'Where they set out to be, Radium Hot Springs.' Adam finished his coffee and pushed the cup away. 'Shall we go into the restaurant and have lunch, or would you rather have a snack here?'

'Neither. I want to get back to Gemma and Gerald.'

'That may not be too easy,' he said slowly.

'Why?' she asked suspiciously.

'I hope you're ready for this,' he drawled. 'They don't want you back with them, Katy.'

'Don't want me back——? I don't believe you!' Her face had gone pale again.

'Your sister's exact words were "You're welcome to her".'

That sounded like Gemma, selfish, uncaring Gemma. Now that they were actually in Canada they no longer needed Katy as a shield to their parents, and so they didn't care what happened to her. 'Did she really say that?' she asked unneccessarily.

Adam's hand covered hers. 'Yes.'

She snatched her hand away. 'So what do I do now?' she asked dully.

'Have lunch.'

'I don't mean now, I mean——'

'I know what you mean,' Adam told her tersely, standing up. 'And you stay with me.' He pulled her to her feet. 'We'll eat in the restaurant, I'm starving.'

Katy hung back. 'I'm not staying with you.'

He seemed unconcerned about their curious audience. 'What other choice do you have?' he said cruelly.

'I—well, I—I could——'

'None,' he answered for her, ushering her into the restaurant. 'I just hope you don't snore. I'm not sleeping too well at the moment, so I can do without that.'

Katy was the one to look about them selfconsciously. 'Do you mind?' she muttered in a fierce whisper. 'People can hear you.'

'What of it?' He saw her seated and then sat down opposite her. '*Do* you snore?'

'No!'

'How do you know you don't?'

'I— Well, I——'

'One of your boy-friends told you, hmm?'

Katy flushed. 'No, they did not!' she said indignantly. 'I just know I don't.'

'I hope you're right. I'm impossible if I don't get a few hours' sleep.'

'You're impossible anyway,' she told him moodily.

He smiled. 'I'm glad to see you're getting back to form. I'd miss it if you didn't have an answer to everything.'

Katy stared broodingly down at the salt shaker as he ordered their meal, sure that she would never be able to eat hers. But when it arrived a few minutes later, a succulent steak, accompanied by french fries and salad, she just couldn't resist it.

In fact she was beginning to feel slightly better as she ate it; the food seemed to make everything look a little better. Even Adam Wild!

'You enjoyed that,' he said with satisfaction when she at last had to give up, the portion too large for her.

Katy flushed. 'Yes.' Had she made that much of a pig of herself? She hadn't thought so.

'I wasn't getting at you,' he read her expression correctly. 'I've dated so many girls who live on a lettuce leaf and black coffee that to see you actually enjoying your food makes a pleasant change.'

'Oh,' she sighed her relief, 'I thought for a moment I'd committed a sin where you're concerned, that maybe you didn't like women who ate too much.'

He eyed her curiously. 'Does it matter what I like?'

'I—No, no, I don't suppose so,' she blushed. 'I just didn't want to irritate you.'

'Any more than you have already, you mean,' he taunted dryly. 'You've been a thorn in my side ever since we met on the plane.'

'But you slept most of the way!'

He shook his head. 'I didn't sleep, I just rested. God, I'm tired!' He ran a weary hand over his eyes.

'Why?'

'Why?' he looked surprised by her interest. 'Why is one usually tired? Because I haven't slept, that's why.'

Katy frowned. 'You said on the plane that you hadn't slept for seventy-two hours. Why hadn't you?'

Adam scowled. 'Why the curiosity? I thought you'd decided the reason. Now that you know me better don't you think I have the stamina for making love that long?'

'Now that I know you better I'm sure that you have. I just don't think that was the reason.' He hadn't the look of a man satiated with love, in fact, beneath the deep tan had been a sallow appearance. 'Had you been working?'

His expression was grim. 'Yes.' He seemed far away, and by his expression his thoughts weren't pleasant ones.

'Where? And at what?'

He seemed to shrug off a burden, straightening his shoulders, the cynical smile once more in evidence. 'Why the interest, Katy?'

'I just thought—— It wasn't very nice, was it?' she said gently.

Once again the mask slipped to reveal a haggard face, his eyes deeply blue as his thoughts went inwards. 'It was bloody awful. I couldn't even begin to describe it.'

'Just tell me where it was.' When he named the place she gasped, her face almost as pale as his. 'Don't say any more. I've seen the pictures on television. Those poor children starving to death . . .!'

'War has a way of doing that,' he said grimly. 'Only the innocent suffer. You should have seen some of those kids, Katy.' His face was anguished. 'Babies, young kids, all of them just dying in front of your eyes.'

'There was an appeal on television. I'm sure they'll get the help they need.'

'It will be too late for most of them. Most of the food is getting stolen anyway. Raiders are coming down from the hills, taking what they need for themselves and then selling the rest on the black market. One child, he must have been about three, maybe older—it's hard to tell, they're so undernourished—he just died in my arms.' He turned away, white under his tan. 'You see, it isn't a question of not finding the time to sleep, I *can't* sleep. That child, he's haunting me.'

'But on the plane——'

'I told you, I was just resting. I got back two days before the flight out here, and during that time I didn't see anyone, I didn't want to see anyone. It was the same on the plane, I was just shutting everyone out, making sure I wasn't bothered by people who either don't know or don't care about those dying children.' A ghost of a smile lightened his features. 'I reckoned without one persistent female with grey eyes and hair the colour of caramel. You made sure I noticed you.'

'Not deliberately.' And she had dismissed this man as an uncaring, selfish brute. How wrong she had been about him! 'Why did you need to take those photographs?'

'Sunday supplement,' he supplied abruptly. He shrugged. 'I'm freelance. I take the work I'm offered.'

'But I didn't know you took photographs like that.'

'You thought I just took nudes,' he mocked. 'Well, I'm over here working and I don't see any nudes anywhere.'

'Except the ones in the camper.'

He grimaced. 'Jud's taste in women isn't mine. I don't like them quite so top-heavy.'

Katy was flushed. 'Gemma and Gerald thought I ought to agree to your offer to photograph me.' As long as it was always from the front; her back wasn't photographable.

Adam's expression became remote. 'I withdraw the offer.' He stood up, leaving the money for their meal on the table. 'Let's go, I intend travelling a bit farther today.'

She almost had to run to keep up with him. 'Don't you think I'd photograph well?' She felt slightly chagrined by his change of mind, even if she knew it just wasn't possible.

'I'm sure you would.'

'Then why——'

He turned so suddenly she stopped speaking. 'I've just changed my mind. Now, let's drop the subject.'

His tone brooked no argument. 'What work are you doing over here?' she asked.

He quirked a mocking eyebrow. 'What do you think?'

'Well, I realise it's photography,' she said crossly, climbing into the passenger seat next to him. 'But what are you photographing?'

'Jasper National Park, mainly.' He drove the camper out on to the highway, seeming to have no trouble driving on the opposite side of the road to what he was used to, unlike Gerald who had scared her to death a couple of times. 'At least, parts of it. And the panoramic view from Banff Sulphur Mountain,' he explained away his presence there yesterday.

Katy frowned. 'That doesn't sound like your sort of work either.'

'I don't have a "sort". I told you, I go where the work is, and right now the beauty of Canada is the therapy I need. Although you're partly right about this job, I'm doing it as a favour to Jud.'

'Jud?' she queried.

'You're a nosy little thing, aren't you?' He gave her an impatient look. 'Jud's writing a book, illustrated of course, about the National Parks in this area. For reasons I would rather not go into, certain of the films I took earlier in the year were destroyed, so I've come back to retake those photographs.'

'Jealous women!' Katy remembered. 'At the airport you said "God protect me from jealous women". One of your women destroyed those films!'

'Which school of detection did you go to?' Adam taunted. 'Whichever one it was it was a good one. Tanya destroyed the films because she thought they were of Laura. They weren't, and she ruined hours of hard work.'

'Exit Tanya.'

'Correct,' he nodded.

'Enter Laura?'

'No,' he grinned, 'enter Katy.'

'Me?' she squeaked.

'Tanya would never believe our being together like this was force of circumstances. She would most likely want to scratch your eyes out.'

'What a charming lady!'

'She had her moments. But I just like to relax sometimes, and Tanya didn't know the meaning of the word. I
told you, I've never yet met a woman I can spend time
with out of bed as well as in it. Most of them just wanted
to drag me off to parties, parade me around as if I was on
show for their friends. They don't seem to know what the
word privacy means,' he said bitterly.

'You've spent time just talking to me,' she pointed out
softly.

For a moment he looked startled, then he smiled.
'You're different, Katy. I was talking about women as
opposed to children.'

She had been going to apologise for making him think
of the dreadful things he had seen in that war-torn
country, but now she just turned away. Every time she
started to like him he said something insulting and she
ended up hating him again.

And it seemed she was stuck with him. She was going
farther and farther away from where Gemma and Gerald
were, and they didn't want her anyway. They were despicable, the pair of them, and she was well rid of them.

'So you really do sulk,' Adam said with amusement as
she continued to seethe. 'I wondered if your sister could
have just been exaggerating. She wasn't.'

To her shame her eyes flooded with tears. 'That's right,'
she choked. 'You make me feel wanted too!'

'Tears, Katy?' he said softly. 'Real tears?'

'Well, of course they're real,' she sniffed inelegantly.
'Just because you're cynical about woment it doesn't mean
you have to be sarcastic to me.'

'If I'm cynical,' his voice was harsh, 'then it's women
that have made me like it. I lived with someone for a few
months once, you know. Another model, her name was
Angel. God, she was the opposite of that!'

'What happened?' Katy asked curiously.

'It all went sour. She was a bitch, a vicious little cat who liked to inflict pain. That isn't my scene, and when I moved out she decided to sell the story of our affair to the newspapers.'

Katy frowned. 'I don't remember it.'

'That isn't surprising, you were probably about ten at the time,' he said disgustedly. 'Half of it was made up, but you try proving you don't do that sort of thing in the bedroom. I've never trusted a woman that close to me since. I'll take them out, I'll sleep with them, but I don't allow them into my life.'

'Are you warning me off?' she asked.

'Did I sound as if I was?'

'Yes,' she nodded. 'Which is rather arrogant of you. I never asked to be let into your life.'

'You seem to be in it.' Adam turned the camper into one of the official campsites. 'We'll stay here tonight and carry on to Jasper in the morning.'

'Are there any shops here?'

'No.'

'But I only have the clothes I'm wearing! I thought I would be able to buy some more when we stopped for the night.' Although it wouldn't be much, she didn't have that much money.

He shook his head. 'Not here. You'll just have to wash your things out and buy some new things tomorrow when we reach Jasper.'

'But——'

'I've driven far enough for one day, Katy,' he told her firmly.

They picked out one of the campsites, fresh logs stacked next to the barbecue.

'Do you have any food in?' Katy asked him.

'Jud left us fully stocked up. I'll light the fire now so that it's going nicely by the time we want to cook our food. Are chops all right with you?'

'Anything, I don't mind.'

They worked together in silence, Adam seeing to the fire while Katy sorted out the food.

'Adam . . .' she said tentatively.

'Mm?' He looked up from adding more logs.

'Adam, I—I won't be sharing—— What I mean is——'

'You'll be sleeping in the same bed as you did last night,' he finished. 'And so will I. I'm not going to force a relationship on you that you don't want. I won't deny that this arrangement would work out better if we were lovers, but as we aren't . . .' he shrugged, 'we'll just have to make the best of it. I don't like unwilling women in my bed, and at the hotel you made it obvious you were unwilling.'

And at Banff she had shown the opposite! Surely he must have realised that? If he had he was choosing to ignore it. 'Well, as long as you realise . . .' she said awkwardly.

'Oh, I realise,' he gave a tight smile. 'You can put the chops on now,' he told her abruptly.

Katy had never cooked over a barbecue before and wasn't making a very good job of it, terrified she was going to burn herself, as fire was one of her dreads. Pretty soon Adam took over from her, his impatience with her uneasiness obvious. She went and sat on one of the bench seats next to the picnic table, her bearing one of dejection.

'Cheer up,' Adam turned to grin at her. 'And come back next to the fire, you'll freeze to death over there.'

It was very cold and it was with great reluctance that she did as he suggested. She huddled down into her anorak. 'Why is it so much colder here than at Banff?' she shivered.

His grin widened. 'Don't you know where you are?'

'No.'

'Athabasca Glacier,' he supplied mockingly.

A *glacier*! No wonder she was cold! 'Charming,' she grimaced.

'I'll show it to you in the morning.' He turned the chops over. 'Watch these while I go and get some plates.'

He made her feel very inadequate, and she glowered after his retreating back.

A girl seemed to appear from nowhere, wearing one of the park's official brown suits.

'I'm collecting fees, ma'am,' she smiled; she was a pretty girl of Katy's age, with wavy brown hair and a lovely clear skin.

'Oh—oh yes,' Katy put up a hand to her own untidy hair. 'I——'

'Here you are,' Adam came out of the camper, handing over some dollars. 'It's a bit colder than the last time I was here,' he smiled at the young girl.

She smiled back in recognition. 'It certainly is. I see you brought your wife with you this time. Have a nice evening.' She went on to the next site.

'Pretty girl,' Katy said nervously, not liking the brooding expression in Adam's eyes.

'Yes,' he agreed absently, moving determinedly towards her. He wrenched her left hand out into the firelight. 'What the hell is this?' he indicated the gold band on her third finger.

Katy snatched her hand away. 'It's only my signet ring turned round the other way. See?' she turned it back.

'Why?' His eyes were narrowed, as cold as the glacier.

'Well, because I—I didn't want people to think we were just *living* together!' Her eyes pleaded for his understanding.

He was unmoved. 'And I don't want people thinking

we're *married*,' he snapped angrily. 'Unless you're prepared to take all that a wedding ring implies. Are you?'

'No,' she hastily denied.

'Then don't make any claims on me, in any way,' he ordered grimly. 'Do I make myself clear?'

'Yes,' Katy said miserably.

CHAPTER FIVE

SHE lowered her head, transferring the ring to the other hand. 'I'm sorry,' she mumbled. 'I only did it for the best,' she added miserably.

'Not my best!' Adam was still furiously angry.

'She was rather attractive.'

'She?' he frowned.

'That girl. I'm sorry if I ruined things for you with her. I didn't realise you knew her.'

Adam sighed. 'I don't. I just met her with Jud. And you didn't ruin anything, she happens to be married to a very muscular Park Warden.'

'Oh!'

He handed her a plate. 'Eat your food.'

'I don't think I'm hungry.'

'Eat it!' he ordered. 'Didn't your mother ever tell you not to waste food?'

Contrition washed over her. 'I'm sorry, I didn't think . . . Of course I'll eat it.' After all he had told her about those starving children she had turned down food! She was an idiot, and wholly deserved his contempt.

The chop was like nothing she had ever tasted before. It was lovely, and she ate every morsel.

'That's better.' Adam's good humour seemed to be returning. 'I've noticed you're always calmer when you've eaten,' he mocked.

'So are you,' Katy returned pertly.

'Maybe,' he acknowledged wryly. 'You can wash the dishes, as I cooked the food.'

She was glad to be able to contribute something, having felt slightly superfluous. She couldn't be a dead weight to him, or he would regret letting her stay with him.

Adam relaxed in front of the fire while she was busy inside, the light having faded to darkness now, and the fireglow leapt across his bronzed features. He looked curiously lonely sitting there, a man totally independent of human warmth. But he was like that through choice, and after hearing of some of his experiences Katy couldn't blame him.

'I'm for an early night,' he said when she rejoined him. 'God, I wish I could sleep,' he groaned.

'Maybe you shouldn't go to bed yet,' she suggested gently. 'Let's talk a while, maybe that will relax you.'

'Okay,' he subsided back on to the seat. 'Tell me about yourself.'

She gave a shy, nervous smile. 'There isn't much to tell.'

'Tell me what there is.'

She told him about her doctor father, about how she was his receptionist. 'It doesn't pay much,' she added ruefully. 'But I enjoy it. I like meeting people, talking to them.'

'You've never worked anywhere else?'

'No.'

'Never really been away from your family before?'

'No.' That was why Gemma's desertion of her to this stranger was so painful to her.

Adam stood up. 'You haven't had much chance to grow up, Katy.'

Why did he sound so angry? 'I'm happy,' she shrugged, frowning her puzzlement.

'But you can't stay cocooned by your parents for ever. You should try to get a little independence.'

'By letting you photograph me nude?'

'I told you I withdraw that offer!' His eyes glittered with temper. 'And any other offer I may have made to you. You're exactly the sort of female I shouldn't get involved with, the home-loving, family type. Before I knew where I was you'd have me married to you and tied to your apron strings.'

Katy half-smiled at this unlikely description of him. 'Only mothers tie you to apron strings.'

'I don't ever remember my mother wearing an apron. It was as much as she could do to admit she had a husband and child. There were always servants to take care of that sort of thing,' Adam said scornfully.

'You were an only child?'

'I was a mistake!' He gave a bitter laugh. 'My mother was furious because her body had to be ruined for nine months.'

'Oh, it isn't ruined!' Katy protested indignantly. 'Pregnant women are beautiful.'

'Are they?' he said in a bored voice.

'Yes!' she insisted fiercely.

'You try telling my mother that. Better still, I'll tell her the next time I see her. It should give her a good excuse to start an argument. We always argue,' he explained carelessly. 'That's why we rarely meet.'

'And your father?'

'Dead,' Adam revealed harshly. 'He's well out of it.' He swung away from her. 'I'm going to take a shower now. Give me five minutes, unless you don't mind seeing a naked man. There wasn't any room in my holdall for pyjamas—not that I ever wear them anyway.'

'I'll give you the five minutes.' Her cheeks were hot with embarrassment.

'I thought you might,' he taunted. 'Don't wander away from the fire,' he warned.

'Are there bears here?' Katy hoped her fear didn't show too much.

'Possibly,' he shrugged. 'So stay near the fire.'

She had every intention of doing so. Adam had revealed a lot to her about himself today, most of it probably without realising he had done it, and she liked him a lot better for knowing what had made him into the hardened cynic he was. She had a vivid picture of a lonely little boy ignored by his mother and brought up by servants, and each successive woman in his adult life had helped to make his disillusionment with the female species complete. At thirty-six there was really no hope of changing that opinion; his bitterness prevented any woman getting close to him even if she were brave enough to try.

Katy could see the outline of his body in the sleeping bag when she went in; the front part of the interior was already in darkness. She took her own shower, washing out her underwear and leaving it on the line in the small bathroom.

'Goodnight, Adam,' she called softly.

' 'Night, Katy,' he murmured.

Once she had turned the light out in her room it was very dark in the camper; the silence was eerie. Katy thought she was going to have trouble sleeping, but she soon found herself drifting off, her troubles forgotten until tomorrow.

When the dream started she wasn't prepared for it; her defences were down. It started quite tamely—the forest, the deer playing—and then they weren't deer at all but a huge bear, a huge dark bear with claws a foot long. And it was coming towards her, nearer and nearer, those claws coming closer and closer. She tried to scream, but her voice seemed locked in her throat. And then her cry broke out, and she began screaming—and screaming—and screaming——

'Wake up, for God's sake!' Rough hands shook her hard. 'Katy, wake up!' an authoritative voice ordered.

Her eyes blinked open, deeply grey, her bewilderment

making her appear dazed. Adam sat on the side of her bunk, his denims pulled hurriedly on, but otherwise he was naked. His dark hair was ruffled from where he had been lying in bed, but he looked just as weary as he had earlier, evidence that once again sleep had eluded him.

'Adam . . .' she swallowed hard. 'I—— It—— I'm sorry. It was the bear.'

He gave a heavy sigh. 'Your imagination has been working overtime.'

She shuddered, collapsing against him. It wasn't until their bare torsos met that Katy remembered she had been forced to sleep naked. She tried to pull away and cover herself, but Adam refused to let her go, and if anything his arms tightened about her. Katy gave up fighting, needing his warmth and understanding.

'It was coming towards me,' she began to tell him, 'on its hind legs. And it was tall and—and so big that—— Oh God,' she shivered with reaction, 'it was awful!'

'I can imagine,' he said dryly, pushing her away from him. 'Will you be able to sleep in here now?'

Her eyes were wide and frightened. 'You won't leave me?' she pleaded, the dream still too much a reality.

'No, I won't leave you. But there isn't room for both of us here, we'll both sleep in my bed.'

'Oh no, no, I couldn't. It——'

He ignored her protests, picking her up in his arms, sleeping bag and all, and carrying her through to put her on the bed over the driving compartment. 'Don't argue, Katy,' he climbed up beside her. 'And you should close your eyes, I'm going to take off my denims.'

'Oh.' She turned away. Adam had only been a vague outline in the darkness, the blue of his denims making his thighs invisible. She felt a movement beside her and knew he had climbed into his own sleeping bag.

'You can turn round now,' he mocked.

He lay back on the pillow looking at her, and Katy's own vision became clearer as she became accustomed to the gloom. She frowned. 'Your sleeping bag is bigger than mine,' she complained.

'That's because I have two zipped together. Now go to sleep.'

'It's very cold, isn't it?' Her teeth chattered.

'Very.'

'You don't want to talk, do you?' she sighed.

'No. I *want* to sleep,' he said fiercely, 'but I can't.'

'Still?'

'*Yes!*'

'I'm sorry. Is there anything I can do?'

'What a damn stupid question! Just stop talking and go to sleep,' he groaned.

'Sorry.' Katy snuggled down under the covers. But she couldn't get warm, the sudden awakening seemed to have made her more sensitive to the cold.

She tried to keep still, not wanting to disturb Adam if he had managed to fall asleep, but it was difficult not to move when she was shivering. Suddenly he moved beside her, turning to begin pulling down the zip on her sleeping bag.

'What are you doing?' she demanded.

'Calm down, Katy. You're coming in with me.'

'I am not!' She tried to push his hands away. 'I'm not getting in there with you!' Oh, it made her senses swim just to think about it.

'You damn well are,' he said grimly. 'There's no point in both of us being awake. Your problem is that you're cold—okay, I'll warm you.'

'You can't,' still she fought him. 'I—I don't have any clothes on.'

Adam became suddenly still. 'That bothers you?'

'Well, of course it does!'

'Okay,' he sighed, climbing down on to the floor. 'Don't move, I'll be back in a minute.'

Katy almost started screaming again as something white and ghostly wavered in front of her eyes. When Adam appeared beside it she calmed down again. 'What's that?' she asked shakily.

'My shirt,' he smiled. 'It should reach down to your knees.' He climbed up next to her. 'You forgot to look the other way,' he taunted.

'You didn't give me the chance to,' she said crossly. 'But you can turn away while I put this shirt on.'

It didn't take her long, and although it didn't quite reach her knees it did go down quite far, the neck gaping open, the sleeves turned back.

Adam peered at her in the gloom. 'Very sexy,' he grinned, throwing back the top cover. 'In you come!'

Katy was glad of the darkness to hide her embarrassment as she got in beside him, feeling his arm go about her shoulders as he pulled her down on to his chest. But still she couldn't relax, conscious of his bare legs next to hers, her arm lying awkwardly across his stomach.

'Lie still,' he growled as she continued to fidget. 'I'm not immune to your—charms, you know. You should have realised that by now.'

'Sorry,' she mumbled, going rigid.

'Just relax,' he sighed. 'Are you feeling warmer?'

'Yes,' she said huskily.

'So am I,' he told her throatily. 'But not for the same reason.' His arms tightened about her as she went to move away. 'Stop being so nervy, I'm not about to leap on you.'

'I'm not comfortable,' she muttered.

'All right, that's it, you've had your chance.' He

removed his arms. 'If you aren't going to try and sleep, I am.' He moved down until his head rested on her breasts, his arm going about her waist. 'Goodnight,' he yawned sleepily.

Within minutes she could tell by the even tenor of his breathing that he had fallen asleep. A feeling of gladness washed over her. Adam needed to sleep, needed to wipe out the bitterness that had engulfed him while he was away. And knowing he was asleep she was able to relax herself, finally falling asleep.

They were even more entwined when she woke the next morning, Adam's legs over hers, their bodies turned in to one another. She had no idea of the time, but she let Adam sleep on, knowing he needed the rest.

The first she knew of him being awake was when his lips probed the softness of her breast. He lifted his head as she gasped. 'Good morning.' Devilment played across his hard features.

'Hello,' she returned shyly.

He placed a light kiss on her parted lips. 'Thanks, Katy,' he was serious now, 'I'm grateful.'

She needed no explanation for his gratitude, knowing that he had slept soundly in her arms all night. 'That's all very well,' she said briskly, 'but how are we going to get out of here?' The intimacy of the close confines of a camper were even more intimate when she shared them with Adam.

His eyes were deeply caressing. 'Do we have to?'

'I—— Yes,' she told him firmly. 'We have to.'

His arms fell away. 'In that case I suggest you get out first. While you're in the bathroom I'll get dressed.' His voice was as cool as hers had been.

That was easier said than done, as the shirt gaped open at a vital moment and gave Adam a clear view down the length of her naked body. That he took full advantage of the opportunity was obvious by his smile.

'Stop ogling!' she snapped once she was down on the floor.

'I was right about that shirt on you, it is sexy.'

'Lecher!' She flounced off into the bathroom, her head held high as she heard him chuckle.

She thought of him as she washed. He was more relaxed this morning, the lines of weariness beside his nose and mouth erased, the pallor beneath his tan no longer in evidence. And she had slept beside him all night! She blushed just to think of it.

'Come on out of there,' Adam knocked on the door, 'or I'll come in,' he threatened.

She clutched the shirt in front of her. 'There isn't room in here for two people.'

'Oh, I don't know,' he taunted. 'It could be quite cosy.'

'I'll be out in a minute,' Katy promised.

Her underwear was still slightly damp, but as she had nothing else she had to put it on. After two days of wear her denims and sweater were beginning to look a bit tatty too. Still, she had no other clothes, so these would have to do.

Adam was fully dressed by the time she emerged, the dark growth of beard on his chin showing that he needed a shave. 'I like my bacon crisp and my coffee black,' he said in passing. 'You'll find most of the things you need in the fridge.' He closed the bathroom door after him.

Katy was left gaping. His good night's sleep had just made his wits sharper. By the time he joined her, newly washed and shaven, she had his bacon crisp and his coffee black.

'You're not a bad cook.' He sat back replete. 'That's two uses you have.'

'Two?' she queried.

'You make an excellent pillow. At least, part of your anatomy does. I never realised how comfortable it was to lie like that.'

Katy's cheeks were scarlet by this time. 'I'm sure you've done it plenty of times before.'

'Sure,' he ate the last of his toast, 'but like Goldilocks found with the Three Bears' chairs, they were either too soft or too hard—yours were just right. 'By "yours" I meant——'

'I think I know what you meant,' she cut in, making a great clatter as she collected the dishes together, 'and I don't care to discuss it. Needless to say it won't be repeated.'

'Not even if you get cold again?'

Her mouth compressed. 'Not even then,' she said firmly. 'Your turn to wash the dishes.'

Katy treated him like a polite stranger once they were on the highway again, expressing admiration for the scenery, even amazement for the Athabasca Glacier which reached almost down to the highway. Adam told her that years ago the Glacier had actually crossed over the road, but that it was slowly retreating.

'Do you want to stay at a motel?' he asked as they approached the town of Jasper.

She thought of the dollars she had with her, of the substantial hole buying clothes was going to make in their number, and shook her head. 'There's no point when we have our accommodation right here.' She used the excuse Gerald had used to Gemma.

'I was thinking of you,' Adam surprised her by saying.

'Me?'

'You're embarrassed about being here alone with me.'

She blushed. 'I'll get used to it.'

His hand gripped the steering-wheel until the knuckles showed white. 'I can't guarantee that every night will pass as innocently as last night,' he revealed harshly. 'Last night I was exhausted, I went out like a light when you held me in your arms, but I'm refreshed now,' he took a deep breath, 'and it's been some time since I took a woman.'

Katy gasped at his bluntness. 'I have confidence in your control,' she told him coldly, not liking the thought of him in bed with some faceless woman—and hating the fact that it bothered her. She mustn't become involved with this man, she would only end up getting hurt, while he would walk away without a second glance.

'That's more than I have,' he muttered. 'But if you're sure that's what you want . . .'

She had no choice! 'I am,' she said softly.

'Okay. We'll be basing at Jasper and taking trips out, if that's all right with you?'

Katy shrugged. 'It's your camper.'

'And it's your damn holiday,' he said impatiently. 'You missed quite a lot by sleeping most of the way up here. I've filmed all of that, it's just Maligne Canyon and Lake that I don't have.'

Katy gave another shrug. 'I've enjoyed what I've seen.'

'That isn't really the point. I'll stop at the places you missed on the way down.' Adam drove into a campsite.

'Wh-when will we be driving back down?' she asked.

'In time for you to catch your plane back to England.'

Her eyes widened. 'Aren't you going home too?'

'Jud's invited me to stay on. I've decided to take a holiday, maybe even stay on for the skiing.'

'Oh.'

Adam turned to smile at her. 'I haven't had any time off for two years.'

'I wasn't criticising,' she prickled.

'Okay,' he sighed, 'so you weren't criticising. It just

sounded that way. We'll book in here for a couple of nights and then drive down into the town. I'll buy you lunch.'

'I can buy my own lunch,' she told him haughtily. 'It's enough that you've been landed with me, I don't expect you to provide me with food too,'

'I offered to buy your lunch, not your body. I don't think the matter warrants this fuss. Accept gracefully, there's a good girl.'

'But——'

'It's only lunch, Katy. If it makes you feel better you can buy dinner and cook it. Deal?'

'Deal,' she agreed reluctantly.

She sat silently at his side while he chatted easily to the girl on the campsite gate, noticing how the girl blossomed under his lazy charm, an invitation in her eyes.

Katy turned away, feeling something like a physical pain shooting through her. She must be mad! Minutes ago she had been telling herself not to become interested in Adam, and now she had realised she was more than interested—she had fallen in love with him! When had it happened? *How* had it happened? He was a hardened cynic, had an arrogant attitude to women that made her blood boil. And she had been stupid enough to fall in love with him!

'You're very quiet,' he remarked on the short drive to the town.

'Am I?' Was that squeaky sound really her voice?

'Yes.' He shot her a sharp glance. 'Are you feeling all right?'

Katy forced a smile to her stiff lips, feeling strangely numb after her recent discovery. She was acting like one of those besotted teenagers she most despised, had let herself fall in love with a sex symbol. 'Yes, fine,' she lied. 'What are you going to buy me for lunch?' She made her voice sound eager.

'Whatever you want,' he returned her smile, visibly relaxing.

She never knew afterwards how she managed to force the food past her lips. And she couldn't begin to tell what she had eaten; her numbness was still with her.

Every movement, every expression of Adam's now seemed more vivid to her, and she was glad she hadn't known of her feelings before she had slept beside him last night. God, to lie so close to him and know she loved him! It would have been beyond bearing!

'Katy?'

She mentally shook herself, and looked up into Adam's handsome face, the cynicism so much a part of him, a cynicism that precluded any woman ever meaning more than a body to him. 'Yes?' she asked dully.

'You've gone very pale, are you sure you're feeling well?'

He would go pale too if he knew the girl he had had wished on him had been stupid enough to fall in love with him! It was pure madness on her part, and Adam wouldn't like it one little bit. To have an affair with her was one thing, to have her bring emotion into the relationship would be another.

'Katy!' he said with sharp impatience.

'Sorry. Maybe I'm still tired. I—I didn't sleep very well.' She had slept like a baby, the warmth of Adam's body had acted like a drug.

'That isn't the way I remember it,' he drawled mockingly. 'By the way, you were right about the snoring. You sleep very quietly.'

'Which is more than can be said for you,' she snapped in her embarrassment. 'You snore like a pig!'

'Liar! I have it on good authority that I don't,' he taunted.

'By one of your women, I suppose!' God, she thought, he had slept with hundreds of women—and she hated every one of them.

'By more than one of them, that's why I consider it good authority.'

Katy pushed her chair back noisily and stood up. 'That's disgusting!' She turned and walked out of the restaurant.

Adam caught up with her seconds later, swinging her round, a dark frown on his brow. 'Why the hell did you do that?' He didn't sound angry, just puzzled.

She shook off his arm, glaring at him. 'Because I'm sick and tired of hearing about your women,' she told him with unwarranted vehemence. 'You talk about them all the time. Don't you ever get tired of boasting of your conquests?'

'Katy . . .' He looked even more puzzled.

'Oh, shut up!' she said shrilly. 'You make me sick!'

'Katy!' He spun her back to face him, and his mouth descended on hers with a savagery that took her breath away. She struggled against him, aware that they were standing in the middle of the sidewalk, people walking past them smiling and staring.

When Adam finally lifted his head her anger was all the deeper. 'Are you satisfied now?' she snapped. 'Does it make you feel good to dominate me with your superior strength, to prove how omnipotent you are?'

'What the hell is the matter with you?' he sounded exasperated. 'We were having a perfectly normal meal when you——'

'Normal!' she repeated scornfully. 'The meal might have been normal, but your conversation certainly wasn't. I don't call your obsession with your sexual exploits in the least normal.'

Adam shook his head dazedly. 'I thought I knew all

there was to know about women, but your sudden changes of mood baffle me. Just tell me what I did wrong.'

'I just did! I don't want to hear any more about your numerous girl-friends.'

'Okay, no more girl-friends. Satisfied?'

'No!'

Katy marched into a shop and began searching through the denims with sightless eyes. Overbearing, conceited—oh, she hated him! She couldn't stay with him for the next week and a half, she just couldn't bear it. If he——

'How about these?' Adam held up a pair of brown corduroys, obviously having followed her.

'I can choose my own clothes, thank you,' she returned with cool politeness.

'Okay, that's it!' His eyes were darkly blue. Suddenly he turned on his heel and walked out, leaving Katy staring after him with dismay.

Had he actually left her here, just gone away and left her? She couldn't believe he would do such a thing. But he had gone, hadn't he? And it was all her own fault! She was behaving childishly, taking her bewilderment over her sudden love towards him out on the man himself. It wasn't his fault that he couldn't be the nice uncomplicated young man she had always thought she would fall in love with. It wasn't Adam's fault that he had suffered one disillusionment after another over women, from childhood to the adult he now was.

She put the corduroys back on the rack and hurried after him. She saw him coming out of a store farther up, and rushed over to him. 'Adam!' her relief glowed in her eyes. She put her hand through the crook of his arm, hugging it to her. 'I'm glad you didn't leave without me.'

'I think being deserted once in a strange country is enough,' he said distantly.

Katy bit her lip. 'I'm sorry about the way I just acted,

Adam. I was very rude to you.'

'You were,' he agreed grimly.

'Will you forgive me?'

He didn't answer the question. 'Did you get your clothes?'

'No. I——'

'Then get them.' He extricated himself from her hold on his arm. 'I'll meet you back at the camper in an hour.'

'Oh, but, Adam——'

'An hour, Katy.' He walked off, his dark head held at an arrogant angle.

She couldn't really blame him, he had tried to be reasonable and she had thrown his offer back in his face. Now he had gone off, to goodness knows where, making it perfectly obvious he didn't want her company.

She bought her new clothes, the pair of brown cords and two extra sweaters, plus two other sets of underwear. It should be enough to get her through, and anyway, she couldn't afford any more. She also bought chicken for their dinner, remembering her deal with Adam.

He was waiting for her as he had said he would be, putting the paperback he had been reading to one side. 'Did you get everything you wanted?' His tone was still cool.

'Yes, thank you.' She put the chicken in the refrigerator. 'Adam, I've said I'm sorry,' she twisted her hands together nervously, 'and I am, very sorry.' She looked at him pleadingly. 'I don't know what else to say.'

'Just tell me what was wrong with you?' The coldness left him. 'Did you suddenly realise that you're in a precarious position alone here with me, is that it?'

Katy licked her lips. 'Precarious?'

'Yes,' he said abruptly. 'Because this morning I told you I wasn't sure I'd let you sleep alone.'

If only that were all! 'Yes,' she eagerly agreed to this

excuse. 'I—— You frightened me.'

'You're safe from me,' he told her harshly. 'You can sleep in your own bed.'

She only wished she could sleep, but it was something she found impossible to do. She tossed and turned in the bunk bed, the cold getting to her again. She longed to be in the warmth of Adam's arms, to feel the long length of his naked thighs against her once again.

She groaned into her pillow. She was acting like a wanton! Even if she did share his bed, let him make love to her, she would just be another willing female to him, another woman to add to his disillusionment.

But she longed to be with him, needed him. Was he sleeping out there, as dead to the world as he had been the night before, his face relaxed and almost boyish as all bitterness left him? She felt sure Adam wasn't aware of how vulnerable he looked when he was asleep; if he did he would make sure he always slept alone. And Katy wanted him to sleep alone if he wasn't to sleep with her, wanted him never to want any other woman.

Oh God, she couldn't stand these tortuous thoughts any longer. She had to get up, get dressed, maybe go for a walk. She thought of Adam's anger the last time she had gone out walking. But this time it would be in daylight, it was almost six-thirty, and she wouldn't need to tell Adam she had been out.

The sight that met her in the living area put all thought of a walk out of her head. Adam was sitting at the dinette, the paperback in his hand, his clothes very creased.

He looked at her with weary, bloodshot eyes. 'Where do you think you're going?'

'I—er——' Katy bit her lips, unwilling to evoke his anger. 'I couldn't sleep.'

'That's obvious,' he drawled. 'You've been moving about all night.'

'I didn't keep you awake, did I?'

He scowled. 'No.'

'Then you—you've been up all night?'

'Yes.' He stood up, stretching tiredly. 'I found I couldn't sleep without my—pillow. I'll get changed and we'll go into town for breakfast,' he added as her cheeks flushed with embarrassment.

'Adam . . .'

'Yes?' he raised one weary eyebrow.

'I—— Nothing. I'm sorry you couldn't sleep.'

'I think it was mutual,' he gave a bitter smile. 'Maybe you need a man as much as I need a woman. Care to oblige?'

Hot colour flooded her cheeks. 'No,' she said huskily. 'Not like this, not like this!'

'I thought not,' he sighed. 'I'll take a wash and then change. Make me some coffee, hmm?'

She did so, willingly. She might not be able to give him herself, but she could take care of him. But he must never know she loved him. Never!

CHAPTER SIX

BREAKFAST was a silent affair, Katy opting for the tradi-
tional bacon and eggs of England, Adam having pancakes
and maple syrup. He ate them with obvious relish, looking
up to find Katy's amazed gaze on him.

A smile lightened his harsh features. 'Don't knock it
until you've tried it,' he mused.

'Pancakes for breakfast!' she shook her head. 'My father
would have a fit!'

'Not healthy, you mean. But there's eggs and milk in
them.'

'And flour,' she derided, 'and butter, and all that syrup.
You ought to be fat,' she complained.

'But I'm not,' Adam drawled.

No, he wasn't, he was lean and firmly muscled. 'I don't
suppose you always eat that much.'

'You suppose right. Jud introduced me to these little
delicacies when I was here earlier in the year. I haven't
been able to get the memory of them out of my mind.'

'They're really nice?' She sounded doubtful.

He grinned at her. 'Fantastic! You'll have to try them
tomorrow morning.'

Katy grimaced. 'I'm not sure my stomach's up to it
this time of morning.'

Adam shrugged. 'It's your loss.' He stood up to pay the
bill.

Katy followed him outside. 'Where are we going
today?'

'Maligne Canyon.'

'Is the lake up there too?'

'It is, but I intend doing it in two trips. I have a lot of

shots to take. We'll make the trip out to the lake tomorrow. You could find it very boring watching me take hundreds of photographs, would you rather stay here and I'll pick you up later?'

And miss being with him for one minute longer than she needed to? 'Certainly not. I'm looking forward to it.'

'I'm warning you, when I work I work with a vengeance. You'll be bored after an hour or so of that.'

'No, I won't,' she insisted stubbornly.

'All right,' he shrugged resignedly. 'But don't say I didn't warn you.'

The road to Maligne Canyon started out all right but after a few miles it became rough and bumpy, although the beauty of the scenery more than made up for this. With the severe weather they had here in the winter it wasn't surprising that some of the roads were in need of attention.

They parked in the car park, then walked down the pathway to the canyon below. It wasn't a pathway as such, more of a mud track with a few rocks to occasionally give a foothold.

Standing on the bridge that crossed over the canyon they could see the Maligne River as it gushed over the rocks before going down through the narrow canyon. Adam stood on the bridge and took numerous photographs, standing in places not really meant to be used for such a purpose, and Katy caught her breath in her throat as he leant right over the narrow bridge to get a photograph of the canyon floor.

He was triumphant as he turned round. 'That should make a fantast—— Katy!' his smile faded as he saw her white face. 'What's wrong?' He moved to her side concernedly.

'You hang over the side of the bridge and then ask me what's wrong!' she snapped angrily. 'My God, you could have fallen over!' she groaned.

'Frightened you were going to lose your driver?'

She glared at him. 'That was a despicable thing to say!' she choked, turning away.

She heard him sigh and then his arm came about her shoulders. 'Stop being so sensitive, Katy. I've done far more dangerous things than hang over the side of a bridge.'

'That isn't the point, I didn't witness them.'

'It's my job, Katy, and I like it. I don't take conventional shots. You don't get anywhere in my profession by taking photographs everyone else is taking, it isn't good enough just to get a clear shot, you need to get the unusual.'

Katy made a determined effort to pull herself together. She was making a fool of herself, leaving her emotions wide open. Adam would regret letting her stay with him if she kept making scenes like this. 'Did you get the photographs?' She forced enthusiasm into her voice.

'Yes. Are you ready to go on now?'

'Of course,' she said with dignity.

Adam led the way, giving Katy even more time to get herself under control.

If she wasn't careful Adam would start to put two and two together and come up with the right answer. And she couldn't take the humiliation of that.

Luckily the pathway here was quite rocky, taking all of Adam's concentration to negotiate, the spray from the canyon making the ground slippery. Where there were no rocks to get a foothold logs had been deliberately placed in the earth, the log steps taking them down to their second bridge.

'Don't worry,' Adam eyed her mockingly, 'I'm not going to lean over this one.'

'You can if you want,' she told him coolly. 'I just won't look.'

He gave a throaty chuckle. 'Spoken like an old-timer!'

'You just carry on and take your photographs and I'll walk over here and look at the canyon from the other side.' That way she could turn her back on him while he did it.

She watched the way the water seemed to be forced through the narrowness of the rocks, boulders forced against the side, the limestone walls eroded into smooth curves. It was beautiful, pagan, and it held her fascinated for several long minutes.

She finally walked back to where Adam was still clicking away with his camera. 'Maybe you'll be able to let me have a few of those,' she said shyly. 'I left my camera with Gemma and Gerald.'

'Give me your address,' he said absently, 'and I'll send you some.'

'It's——'

'Not now, Katy,' he murmured. 'Tell me when I can write it down.'

He cared so little for her he wouldn't even remember her address if she told it to him! 'Are we going on the rest of this walk?' she asked waspishly.

'Sure,' he shrugged. 'Let me go first.'

'I'm perfectly all right.' She stubbornly began walking down the rocky path. 'I'm not incapable——' As she said this her right foot went from under her, her other ankle twisted as she went over, and she slipped inelegantly down on to her bottom.

'What the——!' Adam was beside her in seconds. 'I don't believe it!' he groaned. 'You've done it again!'

Katy's face was creased with pain, her ankle already beginning to throb. 'Done what again?' she asked raggedly.

Adam was checking her limbs, finally coming to the ankle that was beginning to swell up. 'I knew it was too good to last,' he muttered, probing the swollen skin. 'You hadn't done anything stupid for at least twenty-four hours. It had to happen!' He started to sound angry. 'You can't do anything without getting it wrong. Why the hell——'

'Adam,' her calm voice cut across his angry tirade, 'would it be too much to ask you to help me up?' She could see a party of people coming down the pathway, possibly from a coach, and she didn't want them to see her lying on this muddy pathway.

'Here,' he impatiently handed her his camera before lifting her up into his arms, mud and all.

'Adam!' She struggled against him. 'Adam, put me down! What are those people going to think?' she groaned, burying her face in the open front of his shirt as the first of the people began to walk past them.

'Let them think what they damn well like!' His face was grim, his blue eyes scathing as his gaze flickered over her. 'They'd think a damn sight more if I let you struggle all the way back to the car park with that swollen ankle.'

'But it's all uphill!'

'I know that!' he grimaced. But he wasn't even breathing hard, his arms were like steel bands about her. 'How do you do it, Katy?' he sighed. 'Is there some mechanism inside you that reminds you that you haven't done anything stupid for a while?'

'Don't be ridiculous,' she snapped. 'I didn't fall over on purpose. I just——'

'Why is it never your fault? Well, I'm sorry, but this time it was, completely your own fault. I told you to let me go first, but oh no, little miss know-it-all had to prove how clever she is.'

'All I've done,' she said dully, 'is prove what an idiot I am.'

'I'm glad you realise it.'

'I can hardly do anything else when you keep telling

me I am!' her voice broke emotionally. 'Anyone could have fallen on that pathway, it was very slippery.'

'Anyone could,' he agreed grimly. 'It just happened to be you—again.'

'I——'

'It's always you,' he added exasperatedly, almost back at the camper now. 'Who gets you out of these scrapes at home?'

'No one.' Katy winced as he laid her down on the sofa, watching as he took a first-aid box down from one of the cupboards. 'Whether you believe this or not, I'm very capable at home. I have to be, being a doctor's receptionist. It isn't only Daddy I have to worry about, it's his partner too.'

'Is he young?' Adam had soaked a bandage in cold water and was now taking off her shoe.

Katy looked startled by the question. 'Young? Well, I suppose so. Why?'

'Just curious.' He frowned. 'These panty hose will have to come off.'

'Off?' She looked even more startled.

'Yes—off,' he sighed. 'Did the fall affect your head too? You seem to be having difficulty understanding me,' he explained curtly.

Her bottom lip quivered. 'Stop being cruel to me!'

'I'm not being cruel,' he said impatiently. 'Just get the hose off, Katy, there's a good girl.'

'But I can't!' It would mean taking off her denims too, and she would be almost naked.

'Okay, I'll help you,' and his long tanned hands went to the fastening of her denims.

'No!' she pushed him away. 'I didn't mean that I can't do it myself, I just meant I *can't*. Not in front of you,' she blushed.

His blue eyes narrowed. 'Why not in front of me?'

'I didn't mean you especially, just any man.' She was bright red with embarrassment.

'Including young Dr Watsisname?'

'Andrew?' she frowned her puzzlement. 'Of course not, we don't have that sort of relationship,' she told him indignantly. 'Andrew has been a friend of the family for years. He's almost like a brother to me.'

'No man who isn't your brother can ever feel like one. I'll lay you odds on that your young doctor has designs on you.'

His scornful tone angered her. 'And what if he has?' she said crossly. 'He's very nice. He's good-looking, and— and charming.'

Adam half-smiled. 'Meaning I'm not. I must say it isn't a quality I'm known for. Now, are you going to get those panty hose off or do I have to do it for you?'

'You wouldn't dare!'

'It would be far from the first time I've had the privilege of undressing a woman,' he taunted, pulling the curtains so that people outside couldn't see in.

'I already know that. Oh, all right, I'll take them off. But you'll have to turn the other way.'

His expression left her in no doubt of his impatience with such a request, but he turned round anyway. 'Just let me know when you're ready,' he said wearily.

It took her several minutes to struggle out of her tight denims and then her nylons, feeling very selfconscious in just her bikini briefs and a fitted sweater. She cursed herself for wearing panty hose, it wasn't something she usually did when wearing trousers, but as it was so cold she had made today the exception. 'I'm ready,' she mumbled.

Adam turned around, his eyes moving over her quite impersonally. 'This doesn't look too bad,' he probed her ankle. 'How does it feel?'

'Just sore.' His attitude lessened her embarrassment, but

the feel of his hand running down her calf and over her ankle made her shiver with reaction. 'That hurt!' she invented.

He looked speculative but continued to bandage her ankle. 'That should take the swelling down. I don't think there's anything broken, but maybe you should see a doctor anyway.'

'It isn't necessary,' Katy said with certainty. 'Daddy insisted I know some basic first-aid before I went to work for him, and I've picked up quite a lot since then. This is just a sprain, quite painful but not broken.'

'Thank you, doctor!' he responded dryly.

She flushed. 'There's no need to mock!'

He stood back, his gaze not quite so impersonal. 'What would you like me to do instead?'

'Why, nothing.' She was so vulnerable lying here in just her briefs!

'Sure?' His deep blue eyes held her mesmerised, a message there for her if she just cared to acknowledge it.

'Very sure,' she told him firmly. 'You—you wouldn't try to seduce an injured woman, would you?'

Adam grinned at her obvious nervousness, the intimacy of his mood broken. 'I take them any way I can get them.' He laughed outright at the apprehension in her eyes. 'You're quite safe, Katy,' he chuckled.

'I—I am?' Was that disappointment she felt at his casual dismissal of her? She was very much afraid it was.

'Mm,' his eyes mocked her. 'I'm just wondering how I can get the rest of my photographs. You certainly aren't up to walking anywhere for a few days.'

'Go without me,' she said waspishly. 'I want to get my clothes back on, anyway.'

'Oh yes.' He seemed to become aware of her still naked legs. He turned his back once again. 'Go ahead.'

Katy glared at his muscular back, and dragged her

denims on, not bothering with her panty hose. 'Okay,' she said moodily.

He turned. 'What are you looking so annoyed about?'

'I am not annoyed,' she snapped.

Adam smiled. 'Oh yes, you are. There's no better way to get to know someone than in one of these things, and I'm getting to know you very well. You're annoyed with me because I didn't try to get you into bed just now.'

'I am not!' Her eyes flashed her dislike.

'Yes, you are,' he disputed calmly. 'Maybe I would have done, I just didn't think you would be in the mood right now.'

'Don't lie,' Katy snapped. 'You're just worried about taking your horrible photographs—I mean—I——' Oh lord, had she given herself away? She hoped not.

'No, I'm not, Katy. And they won't be horrible photographs. At least,' he grimaced, 'I hope they won't be. I should be past the stage where I make the obvious mistakes.'

'I don't want to hear about your damned photographs! I just——'

'Leave it, Katy,' his face was harsh. 'This just isn't the time or the place.'

'Oh, go and take your photographs! Go on, I shall be all right here.'

'No doubt you would be, but I think I'll leave it until tomorrow. The light isn't too good.'

'Oh well, of course you can't work now!' she said bitterly. 'We may as well go back to Jasper.'

'Yes, we might,' he bit out. 'You stay there.' He started the engine with a vicious movement, and drove out on to the road. 'Your future brother-in-law was right about you—you are frustrated. You need a man.'

'As long as it isn't you!'

'It just could be, if you anger me enough.'

'Then I must take care that I don't do that, mustn't I?'
she smiled sweetly, her sarcasm unmistakable.

Their icy politeness the rest of the day was strangely
upsetting to Katy. She would rather have Adam's sarcasm
than this chilling attitude, rather put up with his taunts
than this silence.

'Adam . . .'

'Mm?' He didn't even look up from the paperback he
had been reading most of the evening.

'I—er—I'm going to bed now.'

'Goodnight.'

'Adam——'

'Goodnight, Katy,' he repeated tersely. 'Maybe tomorrow we'll be able to converse like a couple of rational
human beings. At the moment I need to be alone. I've
never liked people around me, and this is no exception.'

There was no answer to that, and she was so hurt she
couldn't have replied anyway. Adam didn't want her
around. But she had nowhere else to go, was left at the
mercy of his generosity. And he was no longer in a mood
to be generous.

She couldn't really blame him, he had offered her his
hospitality and she had been nothing but moody and
stupid. But did he have to be so nasty about wanting to
be alone, he only had to say and she would have made
herself scarce at the beginning of the evening. She liked to
be alone herself sometimes, and respected anyone else who
felt the same way.

Her ankle didn't hurt too badly now, although it ached
a bit once she was in bed. She hadn't heard Adam go to
his bed, so he must still be on the sofa; his paperback
must be good. She yawned tiredly, wishing she could fall
asleep. It was almost two in the morning, and as far as
she could tell neither Adam or she had been to sleep yet.

She blinked as the door to her bedroom suddenly

opened, admitting a harsh light. Adam stood naked in
the doorway.

'Come on,' he said gruffly, bending to scoop her up in
his arms.

Katy had taken to wearing one of his shirts to sleep in,
something she now felt glad of. 'Where are you taking
me?' she squeaked, envisaging him throwing her out into
the darkness.

'To bed,' he muttered, 'with me.'

'Oh, but——'

'Don't argue with me, Katy,' he looked down at her
with tortured eyes. 'I need you.'

She swallowed hard, knowing the effort it must have
cost him to say that. 'You need me?' she repeated.

'Yes,' and he put her up in the bed, turning off the
light.

Katy's blushes lessened in the darkness. She had never
seen a man in the nude before. Adam had a fantastic
body, firm and well muscled, completely the dominant
male.

He got up beside her, unzipping his sleeping bag and
pulling her inside. Their legs met, their thighs touched,
and Katy could feel herself begin to shake with reaction.

'I—This isn't right, Adam,' she gasped. 'I shouldn't be
here.'

'I haven't brought you here to make love to, Katy,' he
said huskily. 'I can't sleep. I keep seeing that child in my
mind, and I can't stand it! I've never needed anyone
before in my life, but I need you now. Are you going to
deny me comfort?'

'No,' her arms slipped about him, pulling his head
down on to her breasts, 'oh no, I won't deny you.'

He relaxed against her, and a deep sigh escaped his
lungs. 'I hope this works, Katy, because I'm going quietly
out of my mind.'

She caressed his brow with unsteady fingers, wishing she could share his pain and so half his torture. Not many men would be able to confess to such emotions, and she respected Adam all the more for doing so.

'Sleep now, Adam,' she encouraged gently. 'You have your pillow,' she added teasingly.

'Mm.' He settled more comfortably against her. 'You have wonderful—pillows.' Her silence amused him and he chuckled softly. 'I feel better already.'

'Then go to sleep and stop embarrassing me.'

'Yes, ma'am.' All tension left his body and within seconds he had taken her advice.

Katy only wished she could do the same. She had let herself in for a torture of her own, of being this close to Adam, of longing for his arms to go around her and for him to love her. But it must never happen!

This time Adam was awake before her, lying beside her watching her as she started to wake. 'Calm down,' he gently touched her shoulder as she would have struggled into a sitting position. 'How's your ankle this morning?' His hand didn't leave her but slipped inside the V-neck of the shirt she was wearing.

Her breath caught in her throat as his fingers explored the softness of her shoulders, moving lower and lower in soft butterfly movements. 'My ankle is fine,' she told him. It was the rest of her she was worried about! And was that squeaky sound really her voice?

'Good,' he murmured, bending to caress her throat with his lips. 'Because *now* is the time, and this is definitely the place,' he reminded her of his refusal of yesterday.

'But, Adam——'

His mouth came roughly down on hers and stopped all further talk, his hard body half lying over her, his desire almost a physical force. 'I've been watching you for the last hour,' he groaned, kissing her again. 'Has anyone ever told you how desirable you look first thing in the morning?'

She blushed. 'Certainly not!'

'Oh, *God*, I want this . . .' His mouth was fiercer this time, firing her to equal passion.

Adam kissed her intimately, his tongue probing the moistness of her lips, his hands curving about her breasts. His thumbs touched the hardness of her nipples, sending shivers of delight through her body. Her arms were up about his neck, her nails digging pleasurably into the taut muscles of his back. His skin was damp against her, his breathing laboured as he lowered his mouth to her breast, slowly caressing and taunting it with his lips and tongue, his hands firmly on her hips as he pulled her into the hardness of his body.

Katy was sinking, falling into a sensual abyss, her legs entwined with Adam's, her arms straining him to her. She wanted him closer, *closer*. 'Adam . . .' she groaned as his lips trailed across the flat tautness of her stomach and down to her silky thighs.

He didn't answer, intent only on arousing her. He moved up to claim her lips once again, reducing her to a yearning ache, an ache that she desperately wanted him to ease. But he was in no hurry, kissing her, caressing her, making her tremble and shudder in his arms as he raised her to the edge of complete sensual satisfaction.

Suddenly he rolled away from her, staring up at the roof, taking in huge gulps of air.

'Adam . . .?' She gave him a bewildered look.

He gave a deep sigh. 'Neither of us came prepared for something like this, Katy.'

His meaning soon became clear to her and her face blushed fiery red. 'You're disgusting!' She buried her face in the pillow.

'I'm not disgusting at all.' He was out of bed now, pulling on his denims. 'I could so easily have made love to you, Katy, we both wanted it. But would you have thanked me afterwards?'

She swallowed hard. 'Do you usually want thanks?' she bit out.

His eyes narrowed to angry slits. 'I didn't mean those sort of thanks. Use your head, Katy. The repercussions from this morning could have changed your whole life.'

'I wouldn't have let you—you—do *that* to me!' she told him indignantly.

'How did you propose stopping me?'

'I—I could have done,' she said defensively. 'I had no intention of—of going all the way with you, of letting you appease your lust.'

'My dear little Katy Harris,' he taunted, 'you couldn't have stopped me "going all the way" if I'd wanted to.'

'Are you now saying you didn't?' she scorned angrily, the memory of his desire still very vivid in her mind.

'No, I'm not saying that,' he said savagely. 'I wanted you, you know I did. But if I ever have children I don't intend having them this way.'

'I suppose most of the women you know are—are taking something?' she shouted after him as he went to take a shower. 'I suppose they're all sophisticated, know all the rules?'

'They are, and they do. So don't meddle in things you obviously know nothing about.'

'*Me* meddle? You were the one——'

'Yes,' he interrupted wearily, 'I forgot for a while just how innocent you are. But I've remembered now,' he added hardly.

'Let's hope you keep remembering!'

'Don't worry, I intend to.'

They drove down to Maligne Canyon again, and while Adam went off down the trail Katy had plenty of time to dwell on this morning's events. Adam had reduced her to almost begging for his possession—and the worst of it was, he knew it! She would have raised no objection to him taking their lovemaking to its conclusion, would even have revelled in it. Thank God he had come to his senses in time, even if it had been cruelly done.

She spent an hour after Adam had gone trying to get into the political thriller he seemed to find so interesting. It bored Katy, so she put on the radio, a deep depression washing over her as she heard the report of the shooting of the rogue bear. Apparently it was the first trouble of this kind they had had for years—the bear had been down near habitation foraging for food. It sickened Katy that the animal had had to be shot, and she knew she had to get some air, get away from the confines of the camper.

She hobbled her way over to the teahouse, feeling hardly any pain in her ankle. She sat with a cup of coffee in front of her, watching the people as they went in and out, going to look at the souvenirs before they had their coffee.

'Mind if I join you?'

Katy looked up to see one of the coach-drivers standing beside the table she was sitting at, a man of about twenty-four, possibly twenty-five, with blond good looks. He looked pleasant enough. Besides, what could he do to her here? 'I don't mind at all,' she smiled.

'Thanks,' he sat down. 'Are you holidaying? Silly question,' he grimaced. 'What else would you be doing here?'

'It's beautiful, isn't it?'

'Beautiful,' he agreed, his accent definitely American. 'I make this trip possibly six, seven times a season, and I never tire of looking at it. We go on to Yellowstone Park from here.'

'That must be fun.'

'If you get a good crowd on,' he nodded. 'Otherwise it can be a pain in the—— Sorry,' he grinned. 'You're right, it is fun. Are you over from England?'

Katy smiled. 'Am I that obvious?'

'Well . . . 'fraid so. What do you think of Canada?'

'I love it!' Her eyes glowed.

'So do I. I'm trying to persuade my girl-friend to move out here when we're married. She came out with me last trip, it came as something of a shock to her after L.A.'

'I can imagine.'

'Still, I may be able to persuade her yet. Did you hear they got the bear?'

Katy's smile faded. 'Yes,' she said dully. 'It seems a shame.'

'It sure does,' he agreed. 'Especially when it was the guy's own fault he got mauled. I heard he was trying to feed it so that he could get a closer photograph.'

'And now the poor bear's been shot, with a gun instead of a camera. It isn't right——'

'Katy!' a low angry voice growled.

She raised startled eyes, so intent on the conversation about the bear that she hadn't noticed Adam's approach. 'You're back sooner than I expected,' she said breathlessly, aware of the fury in his face.

'So it would appear.' He looked pointedly at the man sitting opposite her. 'I wondered where the hell you'd disappeared to. Aren't you going to introduce us?' He looked at the coach-driver once again.

'I—er—Adam, this is—I'm sorry, I don't know your name?' Her embarrassment was acute. The other man couldn't help but be aware of Adam's anger, of the challenge in his stance.

'Pete—Pete Fresco.' He stood up. 'I hope you'll excuse

me, I can see my party coming back. Nice to have met you, Katy—sir.'

'Sir!' Adam sat down with a scowl. 'How the hell old did he think I am?'

'He was only being polite,' Katy soothed.

His eyes narrowed to blue slits. 'What were you doing talking to him?'

'Exactly what you said, just talking. We were just chatting to pass the time. Did you get your photographs?'

'Yes. I got them as quickly as I could so that you wouldn't be alone too long. I hardly expected you to be sitting in here having a cosy chat with some American.'

'Neither of us had anything else to do.'

'Oh, I see,' his tone was insulting, 'so you thought you would pass the time together.'

'Not in the way you mean!'

'Why not? You were willing to give me your all this morning, so perhaps Pete Fresco was going to be given the same opportunity. I doubt he would have turned you down.'

'You have no reason to think——'

'I'm thinking a lot, Katy Harris,' his voice was grim. 'I'm thinking that maybe you aren't so innocent after all, that maybe you lied to me this morning about not being prepared for something like this. I'm also thinking that you'll continue to sleep with me.'

'I will not!' she told him indignantly.

'Oh yes, you will,' said Adam with determination.

CHAPTER SEVEN

It was very difficult to walk with dignity when you had a sprained ankle, but somehow Katy did it, standing up to walk out of the teahouse. She limped over to the camper, using the spare set of keys to let herself in. If she knew how to drive she would have done so at that moment, would have driven away and not looked back.

Adam had insulted her terribly the last few minutes. And he had hurt her too. That he could think, let alone say such things, hurt her unbearably. He didn't deserve that she loved him, she only wished she could stop such feelings.

He joined her a few minutes later, obviously not having hurried. 'It's no good sulking back there,' he told her once they were back on the road. 'Come and sit in the front.'

'I'm perfectly all right where I am,' she said stubbornly.

He gave a weary sigh. 'Come up here, Katy. Don't make me come and get you.'

'More threats?' she scorned.

His jaw became rigid and he leant forward to turn on the radio, ignoring her completely. Katy heard once again how the bear had been shot, feeling suddenly tearful for the animal—after all, it had only been protecting itself. The man was the one who ought to be shot, for his stupidity.

'Katy . . .?' Adam sounded unsure. 'Katy, are you crying?'

'No.' Her voice was muffled as she hurriedly wiped away the tears.

'You are!' He sounded incredulous, pulling into the side of the road and switching off the engine. He came into the back to sit beside her, his arm about her shoulders. 'What is it, Katy?'

'Nothing.'

'Is it me?'

'No,' she denied quickly.

He gave a rueful smile. 'I didn't think it could be, you should be used to my temper by now. So if it isn't me it has to be the bear.'

'Yes,' she acknowledged huskily.

'You're far too sensitive, Katy.'

'That's better than being *in*sensitive,' she said resentfully.

'Look, I'm as upset about it as you are, I just don't show it as easily. I think the man should be horsewhipped. But they had to destroy the bear, they had no choice.'

'I know,' she sniffed. 'It just doesn't seem fair.'

'Life, or in this case death, rarely is.' Adam stood up. 'Now come and sit up in front with me. We're driving down to Maligne Lake now. We can take the boat trip if you like, although I already have those shots.'

'Your girl-friend didn't destroy those?' She settled in the passenger seat beside him.

'*Ex*-girl-friend. She only destroyed three films, Maligne Lake from the shore will be the last. I'm meeting Jud tomorrow to let him know how things are going.'

Katy gulped. 'He's coming back to the camper?' Sharing with Adam was one thing, staying there with two men was something else.

'No,' Adam smiled, seeming to read her thoughts. 'He's staying with a friend at the moment.'

'A female friend,' Katy said with certainty.

'How did you guess?' he taunted.

'It wasn't difficult,' she told him dryly.

'I suppose not,' he smiled. 'You'll like Jud, we've been friends since university.'

She might find that she liked him, but she wasn't sure she would like him knowing she was staying here with Adam. 'Won't he think it strange that I'm with you?' she asked.

His raised dark eyebrows. 'As I'm usually never without a female by my side he won't think it strange at all. In fact, he tried to provide me with a—a companion, but I refused.'

'Because you prefer to be alone,' she said with remembered bitterness.

'I was angry when I said that, Katy.' His tone was surprisingly gentle. 'You were damned impossible yesterday. I didn't know where I was with you from one minute to the next.'

'Women are often like that. I would have thought you would know our every mood.'

Adam sighed. 'Are you going to be insulting again?'

'Sorry. I—I'm just nervous about meeting your friend, I think.'

'Jud?' He frowned. 'He's pretty broad-minded.'

'But in our case he has no need to be!'

'Doesn't he?' Adam asked softly.

'No!' She evaded looking at his warm blue eyes.

'If you say so,' he shrugged.

'I—— Oh, look, Adam,' she exclaimed excitedly. 'Isn't it beautiful!'

They were driving slowly over a bridge and to the left was Maligne Lake, the water a clear tranquil blue, the deep green pine trees growing right down to the water's edge, the surrounding mountains completely covered in snow.

'It is,' he agreed. 'Even more so now than when I came at the start of the summer. There's more snow now.'

'Maligne,' Katy said thoughtfully as they parked. 'Does that mean what it sounds like?'

Adam smiled. 'It's called "the valley of the wicked river",' he confirmed. 'So named by one of the first explorers here—a woman,' he eyed her teasingly.

She laughed. 'I'm not a Women's Libber.'

'Thank God for that! Apparently it can be very rough here. The river is deceptively mild to look at.'

'And the lake?'

'Well, they have boat trips up it, so it can't be too bad. Put a coat on, Katy,' he advised. 'It's very cold.'

She flashed him a resentful look, but pulled on her anorak anyway. She didn't like him issuing her orders, although he was proved correct about the climate once they were outside. It was freezing!

Adam grinned at her expression. 'Glaciers again,' he explained.

'I see,' she shivered.

'Don't you have anything warmer than that anorak?'

'You know I don't,' she snapped.

He made no reply as they walked over to the low rambling pine building, one of the boats just leaving from its shore. Katy watched as the small craft broke through the clear surface of the lake, sending out ripples to the sides.

'That's a shame,' Adam remarked beside her, also watching the lake. 'There won't be another trip for an hour or so.'

'I wasn't going to bother anyway.'

'We have the time.'

She shrugged. 'I'm not in the mood for a boat trip.'

'Ankle aching?' he queried.

'A bit.'

He frowned. 'You should have let me check it this morning before you got dressed.'

'No!' Her voice was sharper than she intended. 'I—

er—I checked it myself. It looks all right.'

'And you didn't want me near you,' he derided.

She hated him for reminding her of this morning. It had been tempting fate for them to sleep together. But last night he had seemed to need her, although this morning he had needed her in quite another way. He had nearly got her too!

'Did I ruin all your romantic illusions?' Adam was strangely serious, all mockery gone.

'I didn't have any romantic illusions,' she snapped.

'Yes, you did, and they're nothing to be ashamed of. But you would have been ashamed if I'd taken you this morning, and worried too when you realised the possibilities involved.'

'Well, it didn't happen, so let's just forget it.'

'I'm not sure I'll be able to. You—Katy——'

'Adam, is that snow?' she interrupted excitedly. She felt another cold drop on her nose. 'It is!' Her eyes glowed.

He grimaced. 'I told you it was cold.' He hunched over. 'And now it's wet too.'

She laughed. 'Stop being such an old grouch! Isn't it lovely?' she smiled happily.

'Lovely!'

She gave him an impatient look. 'I love it.'

'I can see that. I bet you're one of those people who long for snow at Christmas, too,' he derided.

'And I bet you're one of those people who don't even like Christmas!'

'Wrong—I love it.'

Her eyes widened. 'You do?'

Adam laughed, enjoying her surprise. 'Yes. I just wish the goodwill could be carried through to the rest of the year.'

'I bet it is for you,' she said meaningly.

He lightly tapped her nose. 'Cheeky!'

'Let's walk by the side of the lake,' she enthused. 'You can take your pictures in a minute.'

'Can I really?' he mused. 'How kind of you to tell me.'

She put her hand through the crook of his arm, their earlier rancour forgotten. 'Stop teasing me. We're not in any hurry, we have plenty of time to take a walk first.'

Close to the lake seemed just as blue, the water sparklingly clear. Katy enjoyed their stroll together, felt all tension leave her. After all, she and Adam still had a week to travel together, there was no point in falling out now.

They didn't fall out—but Katy fell *in*! She had been gazing at the beauty of the lake, not really looking where she was going. Whether her ankle wasn't as strong as she thought it was, or whether she just lost her footing, she never afterwards knew. All she did know was that she was suddenly sitting in the icy water, wet up to her waist.

'I don't believe this!' Adam groaned. 'My God, you——'

'Not another word,' she warned fiercely. 'If you dare to say one word about how clumsy I am,' she stood up, shivering with the cold, the water flowing off her, 'I swear I'll push you in!'

'You could try,' he challenged, pulling her out and getting a soaking himself in the process. 'But I'm likely to tan your hide if you do,' he said grimly.

Katy walked hurriedly back to the camper, anxious to get off the icy cold denims. Oh, she was such an idiot! She just didn't know what was wrong with her since she had come to Canada, she was always doing something wrong. And Adam Wild was always around to witness it!

She pulled the curtains, unconcerned with Adam's presence as she peeled off the denims. 'Ugh!' she groaned, shivering almost uncontrollably.

Adam didn't say a word, but moved to turn on the

shower, where the steam soon showed the run of hot water. 'Get the rest of your clothes off, Katy,' he ordered, pulling out towels to dry her with afterwards.

'I——'

'No arguments,' he said firmly. 'You'll catch pneumonia if you don't soon get warm.' He sighed at her reluctance. 'I'll wait outside until you're dressed.'

'But you're wet too!'

'I'll live,' he dismissed. 'But don't be too long.'

The water was very hot, and she stood under it for several minutes. She still couldn't get warm, so dressed as quickly as she could, still shivering very badly.

'Katy?' Adam knocked on the door. 'Katy, can I come in yet?'

He must be frozen out there! She pulled on her sweater and opened the door. 'I've finished now.'

'Thank God for that!' He came inside, rubbing his chilled hands. 'It's snowing quite heavily now.'

Katy looked down awkwardly at her hands. 'I didn't mean to snap at you just now, Adam. I——I just didn't think I could take another one of your sarcastic comments. I don't know how I fell in the lake, things just seem to be happening to me lately,' she finished almost pleadingly. She could take anything from him but a repeat of the chilling politeness of yesterday.

'Whenever I'm around, hmm?' he queried softly.

She gave him a sharp glance. 'Yes,' she admitted reluctantly. 'There seems to be a jinx on me every time I'm near you.'

'I wonder why?' he said thoughtfully.

'I have no idea.' Her voice was much sharper than she had intended. She *knew* why she did these things when she was with him, it was because she was in love with him. 'Shouldn't you get out of your own wet things?' she changed the subject.

'I think so,' he agreed. 'And then we'd both better have a shot of that whisky I gave you the first day out.'

'When I made an even bigger blunder,' she said dejectedly. 'Only a first-class idiot could have got in the wrong camper.'

'You aren't an idiot, Katy.' Adam stripped off his sweater and shirt, his torso bare and tanned. 'A little accident-prone, maybe,' he grinned, 'but you're very intelligent. Why didn't you go in for nursing if you're that interested in dealing with sick people, and you obviously are?'

Katy looked away as he shed his own denims, obviously feeling none of her own embarrassment. 'I didn't have the right qualifications,' she mumbled.

Adam pulled on his dry clothing, not bothering to shower himself. 'Didn't you pass your exams at school?'

'No. I—— My studies were interrupted, and I—I failed them all.' She cursed herself for revealing so much, watching Adam's interest sharpen.

'Why?' His eyes were narrowed.

'I wasn't good enough,' she said lightly.

'Katy!'

'I—I was involved in an accident,' she told him reluctantly.

'Another one?' he taunted. 'I thought you said they only happen when I'm around?'

'This one was different,' her eyes darkened with pain. 'A little girl was killed.'

'Killed . . .? How?' he queried gently.

'A car accident.' Her voice broke. 'She was only seven. She saw one of her school friends across the road and just—just ran out.' Her shivering wasn't all due to the cold now. Once again she could see that little girl running joyfully across the road, completely oblivious of the huge lorry travelling at great speed towards her.

'You said you were involved,' Adam prompted softly.

'I was.' She looked at him with something akin to resentment. 'I ran after her, tried to stop her, but she—she didn't hear me. The lorry—— It—— She died.'

'And you—what happened to you?'

'A broken leg, cuts and bruises.' Her voice was flat, emotionless. 'But she was dead.'

'You poor kid!' Adam came down beside her, pulling her into his arms. 'And I had the nerve to trouble you with my bad dreams!'

'But don't you see, that's why I understood. It's such a waste,' she said vehemently. 'They haven't even begun to live at that age.'

'Neither have you.' Adam gently pushed her long hair away from her face, kissing her softly on the lips. 'Let's go back to town, hmm? Maybe we could even go to the cinema. Would you like that?'

Katy felt a bit like a hurt child being humoured, but she nodded her head anyway, grateful for Adam's gentleness. 'Does Jasper have a cinema?' she asked.

'I think so,' he smiled. 'But I can't be sure.'

It did, just, and they went in to see the cowboy film showing, buying a hot dog when they came out.

Katy grinned at Adam. 'When did you last go to the cinema?'

'About fifteen years ago,' he admitted reluctantly.

'I thought so. It didn't seem like your sort of entertainment,' she explained at his questioning look.

He grimaced. 'I didn't think it showed.'

'It showed,' she smiled.

Adam stopped suddenly, bending to kiss the side of her mouth before carrying on.

Katy ran after him. 'Why did you do that?' she asked shyly.

'Tomato ketchup,' he grinned.

'Oh!' She hoped her acute disappointment wasn't too obvious. She liked it when he kissed her.

The fire in their barbecue was completely burnt out by this time, the evening was very late. Katy got ready for bed in the bathroom as usual, wearing Adam's shirt once again to cover her nakedness. As she came out Adam was waiting for her, still wearing his denims but otherwise naked.

'Goodnight,' she said shyly, and turned to her bedroom.

In answer he swung her up in his arms and once again deposited her in his bed. 'I meant it about you sleeping with me,' he told her firmly. 'We're going to share a bed for the rest of your time here.'

'Adam——'

'I'm not going to touch you,' he promised. 'Well, maybe a little bit. I still need you near me, Katy, and I think you need me.'

'But we can't just sleep together!'

'No one else has to know about it. But I can't sleep without you—someone, sleeping beside me. And you like the extra warmth, admit it.'

'I don't like the passes, though,' she lied.

'No more passes. I'm experienced enough to control any urges I might get in that direction. I've never yet taken a woman against her will,' he derided.

But it wouldn't be against her will, he knew it, and so did she. 'You're experienced enough to make me want you,' she admitted frankly.

'But we both know I won't take you,' he said just as frankly. 'And we both know the reason why I won't. So we sleep together,' he yawned tiredly. 'I'm not likely to tell anyone, Katy. I don't want everyone to know I've been sleeping with a woman for over a week and haven't made love to her.'

Katy gave a shaky smile. 'Not in keeping with your image, is it?' she teased.

Adam did provide extra warmth through the night, but even so she couldn't seem to get warm. And then she came over all hot and had to move away from him, pushing back the covers in an effort to get cool. And then she was cold again, burrowing into Adam's back as she tried to warm herself.

It was like that all night, and Katy was glad when morning came and they set off to meet Jud. Adam had arranged to meet him in one of the restaurants in town.

'You were a bit restless last night,' Adam remarked as they walked down to the restaurant.

Katy blushed. 'I'm not used to sleeping with anyone.'

'Is that the only reason?' his eyes probed. 'You look a bit flushed to me.'

That surprised her, because she felt cold again. She huddled down into her coat. 'I feel fine.' That wasn't strictly true, but she had been enough of a nuisance to him already without bothering him with the strange light-headedness she felt.

'Still cold?' he frowned.

'Mm,' she nodded, repressing a shiver.

'Winter certainly came in early—snow in September. Wait there.' He halted outside a shop. 'I won't be a minute.'

Katy walked up and down while he went inside, feeling warmer while still moving. He was back within minutes, carrying a small paper carrier bag.

'Take off your anorak,' he ordered.

'Take it off?' she repeated dazedly, looking at him as if he had gone mad.

'Mm,' he pulled out a thick cardigan. 'You'll be warmer in this. It's an Indian cardigan, made to keep out the cold. Come on, try it.'

The thick grey and cream cardigan zipped up the front, extremely warm, unbelievably so. 'How much was it?' she asked huskily, choked by Adam's thoughtfulness.

'Don't be insulting, Katy,' he snapped. 'It's a present. Do you like it?'

'I love it,' she told him shyly. 'But I couldn't possibly accept it. It must have been expensive and——'

'And I can afford it,' he finished firmly. 'The important thing is, are you warmer?'

'Much.' In fact she was getting too warm now, beginning to feel uncomfortably so.

'Good,' his arm went companionably about her shoulders. 'Hungry?'

She was thirsty, very thirsty. 'Not too bad,' she prevaricated. 'I really don't think I can just accept this cardigan, Adam. It's too expensive.'

'Consider it payment for services rendered,' he taunted softly. 'Calm down,' he chuckled at her furious expression. 'I meant the use of you as a pillow.'

'That doesn't make it any better,' she said crossly. 'Don't you dare tell your friend that we—that we're sleeping together!' Her face blazed.

'I told you I wouldn't tell anyone, and I meant it. But I think Jud will just naturally assume that our relationship isn't innocent,' he drawled mockingly.

'He will?' Her eyes widened. 'Then I'm not going,' she hung back. 'I'm not going with you.'

'Of course you are. I'll explain to Jud if you like,' he said as she continued to be obstinate. 'Although I doubt he'll believe me,' he added scornfully.

Jud didn't. Katy could see the scepticism in Jud Turner's face as Adam told him how she came to be travelling with him. It was obvious by his expression that he didn't believe a word of it.

Jud shrugged, as if to say, okay, if that's the way you

want to play it ... 'Do you have any idea where your sister and her fiancé are now?' he asked her.

'None,' Katy told him resentfully, knowing he had already classed her as just another of Adam's women.

'I do,' Adam surprised her by saying.

She raised startled eyes. 'You do?'

'Well ... not this exact moment, no, but I do know where they'll be on Monday.'

'Where?' she asked eagerly.

'Here,' he told her calmly. 'They told me to tell you that if you'd had enough of—my company, by then, then they would be here all day Monday.'

'Why didn't you tell me that before?' she demanded angrily. All this time and he had kept something like that to himself!

Adam shrugged. 'I didn't see the point—*we* may not be here by then. We could be on our way back down.'

'But I could book into a motel,' she protested. 'Wait for them to turn up.'

'And what happens if they don't? Use your head, Katy, at least with me you're with someone you know, and I'll make sure you get back for your plane next Saturday.'

'Maybe she's fed up with your—company,' Jud put in mockingly, making the same emphasis that Adam had. 'You may have a reputation as a stud, Adam, but——'

'Jud!' Adam warned dangerously soft. 'Katy doesn't want to hear about that. And neither do I, not in front of her.'

Jud turned to give Katy a speculative look. 'I see,' he said slowly. 'I apologise for my crudeness, Katy. It seems I've misunderstood the situation.'

'It would seem you have,' Adam agreed tautly.

'I guess,' Jud nodded. 'Say how about we go back to Chrissie's place after we've eaten? I would have brought her along if I'd known Katy was going to be here. Chrissie thought we wouldn't want her around.'

'I'd like to see her again.'

'Adam,' Katy cut in determinedly, 'why didn't you tell me about Gemma and Gerald being here on Monday? You must have realised I would have wanted to know.'

'I told you, we may not be here,' he said impatiently.

'You had no right——'

'Not now, Katy,' he cut in firmly. 'We can talk about this later.'

'We'll talk about it now,' she told him stubbornly.

'She's one determined lady,' Jud mused. 'I'll leave you two to chat, there's someone over there I want to have a word with.'

'Stop causing a scene,' Adam muttered as soon as the other man had left them to stroll over to a table just to the left of them. 'I didn't tell you about your sister because I didn't see any point in getting your hopes up. They may not turn up here at all, and then where would you be?'

'Still stuck with you,' she said insultingly.

His eyes narrowed to glacial slits. 'You're lucky to be with me at all,' he snapped coldly. 'I could have thrown you out as soon as I realised you didn't intend being the *loving* companion I had expected.'

Katy gasped, 'You wouldn't!'

'I wouldn't now, no,' he agreed. 'But I could have done in the beginning. After all, I'm not getting anything out of this, only a bad-tempered female who doesn't know when to keep quiet.'

She knew when to keep quiet now, and hardly said a word throughout the meal. She listened to Adam and Jud as they talked about the book, Jud apparently very pleased with the photographs he already had.

Katy's head was pounding, her throat sore, and the hot and cold periods seemed to be increasing. She kept the new cardigan on even during the hot times, not wanting to alert Adam's suspicions. She was very much afraid she was going to be ill, and that was the last thing Adam would want.

She went along with the two men as they went to Jud's girl-friend's house, Katy hardly aware of the surroundings as she was introduced to the other girl. Chrissie proved to be a tall leggy blonde, very attractive, with a beautifully clear complexion and laughing blue eyes. From the amount of male belongings lying about the place Katy assumed that Jud had more or less moved in.

Chrissie must have been in her late twenties, but she looked much younger. 'Do you ski?' she asked interestedly.

'No,' Katy answered gruffly, hoping Adam wouldn't notice the huskiness of her voice. He was a very astute man, and he seemed to know her better than she would have wished him to.

'Katy isn't staying on,' Adam drawled. 'In fact, if she could get away from me now I think she would.'

'Don't fish for compliments,' Chrissie laughed.

He grimaced. 'I'm not likely to get any from Katy. She tells me exactly what she thinks of me. And I don't think she altogether approves of me, or my way of life.'

'No woman would,' Chrissie told him. 'You're a chauvinist. We women are mere toys to you.'

'There speaks the eternal Women's Libber,' Jud taunted. 'She won't even agree to marry me because she says I'd try to absorb her personality.'

'So he just lives here instead—and tries to absorb my personality,' Chrissie smiled.

Katy admired the other girl's forthrightness, noticing the way Adam admired her too. He obviously registered her as an attractive woman, and made no secret of it. Even feeling as ill as she did Katy could feel jealousy snaking through her, and wished Adam would look at her like that. But he saw her only as an inexperienced young girl, someone to tease and humour.

'Only some of the time,' Jud answered his girl-friend's taunt. 'She makes me keep my own accommodation,' he explained. 'Just in case she gets fed up with me.'

'Or vice versa,' Chrissie drawled.

'I doubt that will ever happen,' Adam smiled. 'You have him well and truly trapped. Not that I blame him,' he added warmly.

'I hope you aren't making a play for my girl,' Jud joked.

'I wouldn't dare—I remember how you used to box at university.'

'Katy might not like it either,' Jud remarked softly.

Right now Katy couldn't give a damn about anything, wanting to just sit in a corner and cry her eyes out. She felt terrible, her ears starting to ache too now.

'Katy couldn't care less,' Adam stated carelessly. 'Could you?' he rasped.

'That isn't a very fair question to ask her in company,' Chrissie scolded. 'Would you like a coffee, Katy?'

It might help to ease the tightness of her throat. 'Yes, please,' she accepted gratefully.

'I'll help you,' Jud offered, following Chrissie out to the kitchen.

Adam sighed, giving Katy an impatient look. 'Are you sulking again? I've never known a female like you for——'

Just at that moment Katy fainted.

CHAPTER EIGHT

WHEN she woke she was lying in a proper bed, a luxury she hadn't known for several days. The sheets were cool and comfortable, although she felt very weak, too weak to move. The sun was very strong as it shone across the bed, causing her to blink rapidly.

The bed-springs gave as someone sat down on the bed beside her. 'Katy?'

Adam! Her eyes fluttered open again, lighting up joyfully. 'Where am I?' Her voice was croaky.

'Wait a minute.' Adam sounded almost gentle, bending forward to pour her out some sparkling cold water from the jug on the side-table. 'Drink this,' he encouraged, helping her sit up to swallow some of the refreshing water.

'Adam, I—I don't have any clothes on!' The covers had fallen back to reveal her nakedness.

'I know,' he replied calmly. 'We put some of Chrissie's nightgowns on you at first, but you were in such a fever that we had to keep changing you all the time.' He shrugged. 'In the end it seemed simpler not to bother.'

Katy frowned. 'You talk as if I've been here some time.'

'Three days,' he confirmed.

'Three days! But I—— That means today is Tuesday.'

'Wednesday. This is the fourth day.'

She groaned. 'Then that means my sister——'

'Has been and gone,' Adam confirmed.

Katy's eyes widened. 'You saw her?'

'No. But it's a natural assumption to make. When we didn't turn up they would have moved on.

'Oh God!' she moaned. 'My head hurts.'

'It will do.. Try and get some sleep,' he soothed, smoothing her hair away from her face. 'We can talk when you wake up.'

'But, Adam——'

'Go to sleep, Katy,' he said softly. 'Just rest.'

When she woke up again it was dark, but Adam was still beside her. She smiled at him, not feeling so weak now. She went to sit up and then stopped as she remembered her nakedness. 'Could—could I have one of Chrissie's nightgowns now, do you think?' Colour invaded her cheeks. 'I don't feel comfortable like this.'

His expression mocked her, but he left the room, returning a few minutes later with a flowered cotton nightgown in a pretty shade of blue. 'Come on, sit up and I'll help you on with it.'

'I can do it myself,' she insisted.

He sighed. 'Katy, I've been bathing you and seeing to your needs for the past three days; modesty now is a little misplaced.'

'You—you've done everything for me?' she gulped.

'Everything,' he confirmed. 'Now sit up.'

The nightgown felt cool and refreshing, and she felt more composed with it on. 'Am I still at Chrissie's?' She lay back among the pillows.

'Yes. You've been burning with fever. We had the doctor out to you a couple of times. It was falling in that lake that did it.' His voice had hardened with impatience. 'I should have realised there was something wrong with you, you were too quiet. It wasn't natural.'

'You're still as insulting, I see!'

He grinned. 'You wouldn't know me if I weren't.'

'I think I could bear it.' She closed her eyes wearily. 'Why do I still feel so weak? I'm getting better, aren't I?'

'I would say so. And you feel weak because you're hungry. Ah,' he turned as a knock sounded on the door,

Chrissie coming in with a tray, 'right on cue,' he smiled. 'Katy's just been complaining that we're starving her.'

'I have not! I——'

Chrissie laughed. 'Are you teasing her already?' She put the tray down on the table. 'At least let the poor girl get her strength back.'

'Oh, I couldn't do that!' Adam feigned fear. 'She defeats me hands down when she's up to strength.'

'Liar,' Chrissie grinned. 'How are you feeling now, Katy?'

Adam ran a caressing hand over her shoulder. 'She feels pretty good to me,' his eyes taunted her.

Katy pushed his hand away. 'I'm feeling much better now, thank you,' she said primly.

'See how polite she is to other people,' Adam grimaced. 'She's already been insulting me.'

'I haven't! You——'

'Just ignore him, Katy,' Chrissie advised. 'He's been as worried about you as the rest of us, more so. He hasn't left you for a moment.'

Katy's eyes widened. 'He hasn't?'

'Can't you see my halo?' he mocked.

His taunting rankled. 'If you ever had a halo it would slip around your throat and choke you to death!' she snapped.

Chrissie stood back, smiling. 'She has you all worked out, Adam.'

'She knows me too well, that's the trouble.' He picked up the tray and placed it across Katy's knees. 'Drink your soup,' he ordered.

She gave him a resentful glare. 'I'm not a child!'

'Oh, I know that,' he drawled. 'I certainly haven't been caring for a child the last three days.'

Katy blushed. 'That isn't very fair!'

'Just drink your soup. I'll be outside with Chrissie.'

Her eyes were huge and haunted, deeply grey in her pale face. 'You won't leave me?'

'Of course I won't,' his eyes softened. 'I'll just be outside. I have to eat too, you know.'

'Oh—oh yes, of course. I—I'll see you in a minute, then.' She pretended an interest in her soup.

By the time he came back she had managed to reach her handbag, brushing her hair and adding a light lipstick. She had been amazed by how thin and pale she looked, and just in those few short days. She had little in the way of looks to recommend her now, if indeed she ever had.

'Had enough?' Adam looked at the half-finished soup.

'Plenty, thank you. What did you have?'

'Steak,' he told her with relish.

'Pig!' she groaned.

'With your delicate health you couldn't possibly eat something like that,' he mocked.

'Adam, did you really stay with me all the time?' she asked shyly.

'You shouldn't believe everything you hear.'

'Did you?' she persisted.

He shrugged. 'You're my responsibility, it wouldn't have been fair to ask Chrissie to do it. Not that she didn't offer, but I thought it was up to me. Now go back to sleep, you still look pale.'

'I feel a lot better,' she assured him.

'Good, maybe tonight I'll be able to get a good night's sleep. You've been very restless the last four nights.'

'You didn't have to stay up with me all night.' She sounded haughty. 'I'm sure it wasn't necessary.'

'I didn't stay up, Katy,' Adam said gently.

'You didn't?' she squeaked.

'No,' he shook his head.

'You slept in this bed with me?' she gasped.

'Chrissie only has the two bedrooms,' Adam told her calmly.

Warm colour heightened her cheeks. 'So they know you've been sleeping with me,' she said dully.

'They assumed I was anyway. We argue like lovers, Katy, haven't you realised that?'

'We argue because we don't like each other,' she told him heatedly.

'Now you know that isn't true,' he touched her hair. 'You said some very revealing things in your delirium.'

Her eyes widened with trepidation. 'I did?'

'Enough to tell me you didn't mind me in bed with you. I'm too much of a gentleman to tell you what you said, but——'

'You aren't a gentleman at all,' Katy snapped, 'Or you wouldn't even have mentioned it.'

'Maybe not. It's eleven o'clock, it's time you went to sleep, young lady.' He began taking off his shirt.

'Adam——' she bit her lip, accepting that he intended sleeping here. 'Adam, why don't you ask me about it?' She had been expecting his questions ever since he had told her he had been bathing her, and yet he had said nothing.

He raised his eyebrows, his torso golden in the lamplight. 'About what?'

She sighed. 'I know you must have seen them. If you've been caring for me then you must have seen the scars on my back.'

'Yes,' he acknowledged. 'But I figured that if you'd wanted me to know about it you would have told me. We have few secrets from each other.'

That was true; she had talked intimately with this man, revealed so much to him. And he had been equally frank with her. 'It happened in the accident,' she told him. 'The one where the little girl died.'

Adam frowned as he got into bed beside her. 'But I thought you had a broken leg, cuts and bruises? Those scars were caused by——'

'Fire,' she nodded, snuggling against his chest as he put his arm about her. 'After hitting me the lorry crashed into a tree, the petrol tank exploded, and my clothing caught fire. So you see,' she said in a choked voice, 'even the body isn't perfect.'

'It is to me,' he growled. 'More than perfect. I know every single inch of you, including the scars, and I still desire you. Katy . . .' he turned towards her. 'Katy, I want you,' he groaned.

His lovemaking was like a torrent, sweeping all before it, crushing Katy against him until she had to cry out. At once his ardour gentled, becoming a slow sensuous tide, rising like the sweet crescendo of a wave, taking them farther and farther away from sanity.

'Oh *God*!' he finally groaned, throwing himself away from her. 'What sort of animal am I?' He looked at her with tortured eyes. 'I disgust myself. You've been ill, seriously ill,' he got out of bed to pull on his denims and a sweater, 'and as soon as you start to feel slightly better I try to make love to you!'

Katy watched as he walked towards the door, her senses still swimming. 'Where are you going?' she asked dazedly.

'For a walk. And I won't be sharing your bed. If you're feeling better tomorrow we may leave for Calgary.'

'Adam . . .' But he had already gone.

And he didn't put in an appearance the next morning either. Chrissie brought in the doctor, and he proclaimed her well enough to travel the next day, as long as she didn't overdo it.

'Where's Adam?' she asked Chrissie as they sat in the lounge drinking coffee. She still felt slightly weak, but other than that felt quite well; her appetite was returning.

'He went back up to Maligne Lake, he and Jud. Adam said he didn't get the pictures of the lake he wanted.'

'No,' Katy said ruefully. 'I fell in before he had the chance.'

'So he said,' the other girl nodded.

Katy gave a derisive smile. 'I suppose you think I'm an idiot, too?'

'Too?'

'Adam's always calling me one.'

'He doesn't mean it. You worry him, and Adam doesn't like that,' Chrissie told her.

'Why?'

'Because it means he cares. You should know by now that Adam doesn't accept emotions as other men do. He's shut people out for so long now that he resents any dent in his armour.'

'And I'm a *dent*?' Katy asked humorously.

Chrissie grimaced. 'I'm afraid so. He's been in the foulest mood since yesterday.'

'More foul than usual, you mean?'

'His mood is usually pretty even. He doesn't usually allow anyone close enough to him to upset him. His cynicism overlies everything he does.'

'You seem to know him well,' Katy commented in surprise.

'I knew him in London years ago. That was how I met Jud.'

'I see.'

'I don't think you do,' Chrissie denied gently. 'Adam was dating my sister, not me. She's married now, with a couple of kids, but she still has fond memories of Adam.'

'He has that effect,' Katy agreed huskily.

'Does he know you love him?'

'No! No, he doesn't,' she said more calmly. 'If he did he would get rid of me as soon as he could. Adam has affairs, he doesn't fall in love, mainly because he doesn't even believe it exists. Not that I blame him, he's had some bad experiences with women in the past.'

'He's told you about them?'

'Yes,' Katy nodded.

'Then you aren't a dent at all, you're a crater. Adam never discusses his private life, not even with Jud, and they have been friends for years.'

'I think it was just a case of having little else to do while we've been travelling together.'

'Really?' Chrissie laughed. 'A handsome specimen of manhood like Adam and all you could think of to do was talk?'

'I didn't mean it that way,' Katy blushed.

'I know. Would you like more coffee?'

'No, thanks.' Katy felt grateful for the other girl's sensitivity. 'Do you have any idea when they'll be back from Maligne Lake?'

Chrissie shrugged. 'They didn't say. Adam decided not to go to Calgary today, but I should think they'll get back before dark.'

The two men arrived back shortly before dinner, Adam making a polite enquiry about Katy's health, expressing satisfaction when told she was well enough to travel. Katy felt deeply hurt by his attitude, knowing he would be glad to leave her at her hotel on Saturday.

'I should get an early night,' he told her after they had eaten, his tone cool. 'We'll be leaving early tomorrow, straight after breakfast in fact.'

She stood up obediently. 'Will you be long?' she asked shyly.

'Will I——?' he scowled. 'I told you last night, Katy,' he snapped coldly, 'I'm not going to sleep with you again. Goodnight.'

'You—you bastard!' she choked, running into the bedroom and slamming the door.

Chrissie and Jud had looked so taken aback when Adam had spoken to her in that way, and no wonder; he had been deliberately cruel and hurtful. Katy couldn't face them again, couldn't bear to see the pity in their eyes.

Her choked sobbing drowned out the sound of the door opening and the footsteps of the man now standing beside the bed. But something warned her of his presence there, and she looked up with a tear-stained face.

'Jud and Chrissie tell me I was a little hard on you,' he said curtly, his eyes glacial.

'And that's why you're in here,' she cried. 'You enjoyed talking to me like that in front of them, you enjoyed humiliating me. Get out of here! Go on, get out!'

Instead Adam grasped her wrists, pulling her up so that her face was within inches of his. 'Would you rather I stayed here with you?' he bit out forcefully. 'Would you rather I shared that bed with you tonight? Made love to you? Used you as you're begging to be used?'

'No!' She turned away from the contempt in his face. 'I just want you to leave me alone.'

'Leave you alone? What the hell do you think I've been trying to do?' he rasped, furiously angry as he threw her roughly down on the bed. He moved to pace the room. 'Do you think I enjoy sleeping on the sofa in the lounge? That I like sleeping out there when there's a bed and a willing woman in here? It's bloody agony!' he groaned. 'But a girl like you doesn't want the sort of relationship I'm capable of.'

'How do you know that?' she choked.

'I know,' he said grimly. 'My sort of relationship is brief, very brief in some cases, and you're the sort of girl marriages are made of.'

'I could settle for less, if I loved someone.'

'Love!' he scorned cruelly. 'The most abused word in the history of mankind! Between a man and a woman it comes down to a much baser emotion. You once told me I lust after you—well, I do, but I've lusted after hundreds of other women, in exactly the same way. You talk about love too easily, Katy. You don't even know me. No, you don't,' he snapped as she went to protest. 'You don't know *me*, you just want my body in the same way I want yours, but that isn't *love*. Chrissie and Jud have the nearest thing I've ever seen to love, the sort of love that allows each partner freedom, the sort of love that keeps them together even though they both know they could be free. Marriage is a love-wrecker, only freedom can give you love, the freedom to choose whether to go or whether to stay.'

'If you want me to live with you——'

'I don't,' he told her coldly. 'You see, I love being free, of everyone and everything. I belong to no one and no one belongs to me.'

'But if someone loves you——'

'No one does,' he said firmly. '*You* don't. You've experienced sexual excitement in my arms and you prefer to think of it as love. It isn't. I could make love to you now, and in a couple of hours I may want to take you again, but the time in between I just wouldn't want to know. Women are bodies to me, faceless, nameless bodies. Do I make myself clear?'

'Very,' she mumbled.

'Good!' and he slammed out of the room.

He might as well have hit her. His words had been calculatedly cruel, her offer of love thrown back in her face. Not that she had actually told him she loved him, but he had guessed that was what she meant. His reaction had been as she had told Chrissie it would be, he intended ejecting her from his life as soon as possible.

That became even more apparent the next day when

he told her he intended driving straight through to Calgary in one day.

'But it will take hours,' she protested, huddled down in the warmth of the cardigan he had bought her.

She had known of Chrissie and Jud's sympathy as they had made their goodbyes, had known of it and hated it. Adam was more remote than ever, his face harsh in the morning sunlight.

'I'm driving straight through,' he repeated his intent.

'Are you so anxious to get rid of me?'

'Yes!'

She drew a ragged breath. 'Then just keep on driving. Why should I care if you exhaust yourself?'

'Why indeed?' he said grimly.

It seemed like years ago that she had met Adam on the plane, had looked at the man at her side and decided he was the hardest man she had ever seen, a man of pure granite. How true that had turned out to be!

'Lunch?' He had stopped at the same restaurant as they had on the way up, the turn-off to Red Deer a few yards down the highway.

Katy didn't feel as if she could eat a thing, but the doctor had told her she must eat now the fever had passed, that she had to build her strength up. 'Lunch,' she agreed tersely.

'If you give me your address,' Adam told her over their meal, 'I'll have those photographs sent on to you.'

'You needn't bother,' she answered curtly, pushing her half-eaten meal away. 'If I need reminding of this holiday I can always look at my sister's snapshots.'

'But you would rather not be reminded, hmm?' Adam said dryly.

'Much rather not,' Katy agreed.

'Chalk it down to experience. Every girl is entitled to one fling in her lifetime. I'm sure that if you tell

Andrew nothing happened between us that he'll believe you.'

'Andrew?' she frowned. 'Why should I tell him anything?'

'I thought he was interested in you?' Adam taunted.

'Maybe he is,' she defended, clinging to her pride. 'But I won't need to tell him that nothing happened between us, he knows me well enough not to need to ask.'

'He does?' He shrugged. 'How easily some men are fooled!'

'But nothing did happen,' she protested.

'Nothing?' he asked softly. 'So you could freely tell Andrew everything that's taken place while you've been with me? Would have no qualms about telling him we shared a bed——'

'Quite innocently,' she cut in.

'Not always,' his eyes mocked. 'In fact, hardly ever. We could have been lovers the whole of the time we've been together, and there wouldn't have been any objections from you.'

'Oh, wouldn't there? Well, let me tell you——'

'Don't tell me anything, Katy,' he put his hand over hers. 'I think we've said all we need to about our feelings for each other.'

'Feelings!' Katy shook off his hand and stood up. 'You don't have any feelings, except basic ones. You're like a robot. You charm women, you make love to them, then you throw them out of your life. Well, I want more from a man than an accomplished lover. I admit I may briefly have been infatuated with you, but Andrew is worth ten of you!' And she walked out of the restaurant.

Adam followed a few minutes later, getting into the vehicle and driving on in silence. The terrible clunking noise in the engine about five minutes later heralded the start of the trouble, finally getting so bad that Adam had to drive on to the hard shoulder, the noise getting louder all the time.

'That's all I need,' he muttered, swinging out of the cab to look in the hood.

'What's the matter with it?' Katy got out and stood beside him.

He gave her a silencing glare. 'How the hell should I know?' He slammed the hood back down. 'Give me a camera and I can spot what's wrong with it straight away, with an engine I have no chance.'

Katy looked at the long stretch of road either way, no sign of habitation anywhere in sight. 'What do we do now?'

'*We* don't do anything,' he said pointedly. 'I hitch a lift back to the gas station and hope they get a mechanic out straight away.'

'And if they can't?' She didn't relish the idea of being left here on her own.

'Then I come back here and wait until they can send someone,' he replied impatiently.

'Couldn't I come with you?' she asked hopefully.

'No point,' he refused callously. 'Besides, someone ought to stay with the vehicle. I shouldn't be long.' He crossed over the highway, flagging down a car as it came towards him.

Katy watched the ease with which he chatted to the man before they drove off. Adam did not give her a second glance, his harsh profile turned firmly away from her.

Quite a few other vehicles drove past the camper, one man even stopped to ask if he could be of any assistance. Katy thanked him for his concern but explained that her—her friend had gone for help.

It was almost an hour later when Adam arrived back, brought by another helpful driver before he drove on.

'Couldn't anyone come?' she asked needlessly. It was

obvious that no mechanic had come!

'About another hour,' Adam replied tersely. 'They're already out on a job. Let's hope they're no longer than that,' he scowled.

'We won't be able to get to Calgary today,' she remarked thoughtfully.

'No,' he acknowledged grimly. 'But if they aren't too long, and the repairs are easy, we may be able to get to Lake Louise and book into a motel there.'

'A motel?' Katy frowned. 'But——'

'I'm not sleeping in the camper with you,' he told her bluntly.

'I see,' she bit her lip. 'I just thought it seemed silly when we——'

'It would be even sillier to stay in here. Believe me,' he added harshly, 'it would be sheer stupidity on your part. I'll only keep saying no for so long, and then God help you. And me,' he groaned, running a weary hand through his hair. 'I've had two lousy nights' sleep.'

'Bad dreams?' she asked gently.

'Of a different type,' he nodded. 'I need a woman, Katy, any attractive woman will do. *That*'s why we're going to a motel, because you aren't just any woman. I respect you, Katy, and that's something that doesn't happen too often. If I should do anything to spoil that idealistic idea you have of love then I think I'd want to kill myself. To take someone's dreams away from them is to destroy that person. Everyone has their dreams.'

'Except you,' she put in quietly.

'Even me once.'

'And someone took them away and destroyed you.' The sensitive part anyway.

'Something like that,' he agreed curtly. 'Ah, good, here comes the mechanic. Let's hope it doesn't take too long.'

It didn't, only half an hour or so; the technical terms

were beyond Katy as the young boy told Adam what had been wrong with it. She knew by the amused glitter in his deep blue eyes that it was beyond him too.

Katy wished they weren't going to stay at a motel for the night. Tomorrow Adam would leave her at her hotel and she would probably never see or hear from him again. Admittedly he had said he would send her some photographs if she gave him her address, but a formal letter from his secretary wasn't the sort of contact she wanted from him. The contact she wanted was much more physical, one night with Adam that would have to last her a lifetime. He wouldn't be taking away her dreams if he gave her that night, he would be making her dreams come true.

'Do you want to see the lake?' he indicated the sign for Peyto Lake. 'It's worth seeing, if you feel up to the walk.'

Anything to delay her final parting from him. 'I'd love to,' she agreed eagerly.

It was quite a walk up to the lake, all uphill, but the final view was worth it. Peyto Lake nestled between the mountains far below them, a long expanse of water, the most gorgeous blue Katy had ever seen, almost an unreal blue.

They went on to the wooden viewing area. 'Why is it that colour?' she asked Adam.

'Silt from the glaciers settles on the bottom of the lake and the water reflects off it. Beautiful, isn't it?'

'Very,' she agreed, unable to take her eyes off it.

'You're looking pale,' Adam frowned down at her. 'I shouldn't have brought you up here,' he said impatiently. 'You're still ill, you only got up yesterday.'

'I'm——' She was about to deny any feeling of weakness and then she hesitated. Maybe this was another way of delaying them. 'I am feeling a bit faint,' she amended.

'Oh, hell!' he muttered angrily. 'Okay, let's get down

from here.' He put an arm about her waist to support her on the walk down.

Katy leant against him weakly, welcoming this contact with him. The walk down was much easier, but she wasn't going to tell Adam that, and smiled wanly when he asked how she felt. She liked his concern, revelled in it, almost feeling bereft when they reached the bottom and his arm left her waist.

'Adam . . .'

'Mm?' he looked up from putting the key in the ignition.

'Adam, I—I don't feel well.' It wasn't far from the truth, she did feel a little shaky, but that was probably from being held in his arms.

He sighed. 'Get into the back and lie down.'

'I—er—Could we stop soon, Adam? The camper is making me feel sick today.' She had her fingers crossed behind her back as she told this lie.

He gave her a suspicious look, but her expression remained bland. 'You really don't feel up to travelling any farther?' he asked slowly.

'No,' she said huskily.

'Okay,' he shrugged. 'There's a campsite a few miles ahead. We——'

'What about the one we just passed? That isn't far at all.'

'It's in the wrong direction,' he dismissed.

'But nearer, surely,' she was checking the map. 'It only looks half the distance,' and it was also a step backwards.

'I don't see why the hell I can't just drive straight through while you rest in the back.'

'You can if you want,' she accepted dully. 'I suppose I'll be all right.'

Adam sighed. 'No, we'll go back to the campsite. I think what you need more than anything is some food inside you. You didn't have any breakfast, and you hardly touched your lunch.'

'You're probably right,' she agreed almost eagerly. 'In fact, I'm sure you are. I could just eat a nice juicy steak.'

'A light diet, the doctor said,' Adam reminded her dryly.

'All right, a little steak,' she compromised teasingly.

His expression lightened and he looked more like the old Adam. 'I don't think that's quite what the doctor had in mind.'

Katy pouted at him, feeling more relaxed with him. 'But I'm hungry, Adam,' and surprisingly she was. She would have Adam to herself tonight, and that was enough to give her an appetite.

'So am I,' he smiled fully now. 'Okay, Wildfowl Lake, here we come!'

CHAPTER NINE

ADAM insisted that she sit down and take things easy while he cooked the steaks, so Katy sat outside and watched him. The evening was clear and fresh, the—— Her breathing came to a halt as she saw a bear lumbering out of the trees towards them.

'A—A——' She couldn't speak, couldn't move, as her nightmare became a reality. 'Adam!' she finally managed to squeak. 'Adam, it's a bear!'

He froze. 'Where?' his voice was soft, controlled.

'B-behind you.' Her teeth started to chatter, her whole body shaking.

He turned slowly, picked up the grill with the steaks on. 'Walk slowly towards the camper,' he ordered as the bear began sniffing the ground a few yards away from them.

'I—I can't!' She was frozen to the spot.

'Move, damn you!' he said forcibly.

Katy moved, slowly as he had told her to, her stricken gaze locked on the bear. At the last she would have faltered and fallen, but Adam hurriedly pushed her inside and closed the door behind them.

'Oh, Adam!' She was shaking so much she couldn't stop. 'I—I was petrified.'

He pulled her against him. 'It's all over now. Let's see what he's up to, hmm?'

Katy recoiled. 'I'm not going out there!'

'We'll look out of the window, silly,' he teased lightly. 'Come on.'

The bear was just ambling through the camp, walking on all fours across the road and into the trees on the other side. The denseness of the forest swallowed up the darkness of the bear and it was as if he had never been.

'Well?' Adam said tauntingly. 'What did you think of your first bear?'

'I was terrified,' Katy choked. 'But he—he was rather magnificent, wasn't he?'

'And free,' he reminded her. 'That's what I like about this part of the country. I'll go back out and finish cooking the steaks now.'

She looked over to where the bear had recently disappeared. 'Are you sure it's safe?'

'He won't be back. But if you're nervous you can stay in here.'

Katy followed him outside, feeling totally miserable about Adam's further reference to freedom. To him it meant everything.

'Eat your steak,' Adam ordered as she remained deep in thought.

They retired early, Adam to his bed, Katy to hers, Adam informing her they would be making an early start in the morning. She had known by the determination in his face that he wouldn't welcome any suggestion from her that they share his bed. But she wanted him, *needed* him.

She heard a faint rustle of sound, and turned over expectantly. Adam had come to her after all. She couldn't go to him, she couldn't take his rejection of her one more time, but if he came to her it was a different matter.

'Adam . . .?' she queried softly as he made no comment.

Still the rustling noise continued. She got out of bed, picking up the torch Adam had given her and softly opening the door to shine the light outside into the living area. She couldn't see Adam at all, but she could see something else—a mouse!

'Adam!' she screamed, terrifying the life out of the mouse as it ran into a cupboard. 'Adam!' she shuddered, a creature she had always thought soft and furry now taking on a frightening aspect.

'What the hell is the matter with you now?' he growled, suddenly out of the darkness. 'If this is some plot of yours to get me into bed with you——'

'You conceited swine!' His attitude after her fright made her angry. 'I don't want to sleep with you! We have a mouse in the camper.'

He switched the light on, still in his denims and thick sweater, slightly creased now. 'You saw it?' His eyes were narrowed.

'Well, of course I saw it!' she said impatiently. 'It was just sitting there looking at me. It went into the cupboard under the sink.'

She cringed as Adam began hunting through the cupboard, coming up with nothing. 'You're sure it went in here?' He turned to look at her.

'Yes,' she gave a vigorous nod.

He stood up, closing the cupboard door. 'Well, it's gone now, probably out the way it got in. I should have taken that rubbish out when I had the chance, that must have been what attracted it in here.'

Katy knew he was rebuking her. He had wanted to take the debris from their meal over to the bear-proof rubbish container, but she had pleaded with him not to go because she was terrified the bear would come back and attack him.

She sat down on her bed, shivering. 'I can't go back to sleep now. He might come back in once we turn off the lights.'

'Doubtful. But I can't sleep either.'

She knew that, knew by his clothing that he hadn't

slept. 'So what do we do now?' She looked at him almost hopefully.

'There's only one thing we can do.'

'Yes . . .?'

'We drive on,' Adam told her grimly.

'Now?' she gasped. 'In the dark?'

'Why not?' he shrugged. 'I would prefer to be driving rather than just sitting here waiting for daylight.'

Katy gave him a shy glance. 'We don't have to just sit here.'

His blue gaze ripped into her, leaving her in no doubt of his anger. 'Stop acting like a whore,' he snapped. 'If I'd wanted you I would have taken you, God knows you've given me enough encouragement. But I don't want you or any of the ties you would put on me. So we drive on. Any objections?'

'None,' she choked.

While Adam drove she dressed, the black silence all around them making everything seem unreal, making this whole situation seem unreal. It seemed like a lifetime since she had sat beside him on the plane trading insults with him, seemed like years since he had told her she was worth photographing—something he now knew was impossible, with the scars she had. The scars——!

'Adam . . .' she began hesitantly. 'Adam, was it my scars that put you off?'

'Scars?' he frowned. 'Oh, you mean the ones on your back. Nothing put me off, Katy, except that you are the person you are.'

'But the scars *are* unsightly.'

'I already told you, they mean nothing to me. God, didn't my actions two days ago, even after I'd seen the scars, more than prove that?'

'But you're used to perfection,' she played with a seam on her denims, 'used to——'

'Damn what I'm used to!' he snapped forcefully. 'I'm sorry,' he muttered, 'I didn't mean to shout. Let's just drop the subject. You are what you are, I am what I am, and never the twain shall meet.'

'But we have met,' she pointed out.

'Pure fluke,' he dismissed. 'If there'd been a first class seat on that plane we would never have spoken to each other.'

'I wouldn't have liked that,' she admitted softly.

'I seem to remember you called me sarcastic, that you even turned your back on me a couple of times.'

'You were sarcastic,' Katy accused. 'And you were awful at the hotel too.'

'Wasn't I?' he grinned at her.

'Dreadful. Gemma accused me of all sorts of things the next day. Oh, my God—Gemma!' she exclaimed in horror. 'I've got to face her later today. You'll stay with me until then?' She looked at him pleadingly.

'I——'

'Oh, please,' she begged as she knew he was about to refuse. 'Gemma can be—well, she——'

'Can be a bitch,' he finished grimly. 'I've already gathered that. Okay, I'll stay with you until you meet up with your sister. But after that I intend driving straight back to Jasper.'

They drove straight to the hotel when they reached Calgary, going in for breakfast before going for a walk around the town. Katy had already bought her presents for the people at home, but she bought a leather wallet for Adam, and gave it to him once they had returned to the hotel.

'I can't take this, Katy——'

'Oh, please, I want you to.'

'I didn't expect——'

'I know you didn't,' she cut in awkwardly. 'But I

wanted to buy you something. If you don't like it——'

'I like it,' he said huskily, holding out a small parcel to her. 'I bought you this in Jasper.'

When she unwrapped it it was to find one of the small jade bears she had so admired in one of the shops.

'Of course,' Adam added ruefully, 'that was before you had your fright yesterday.'

'It's beautiful, Adam!' There were tears in her eyes. 'I'll keep it always.' A treasured possession from the man she loved. 'I'll never forget this holiday,' she smiled tremuously.

Adam gave a husky laugh. 'With the disasters you've been through I think you'll have trouble forgetting it.'

She never wanted to; she would cherish every minute spent in Adam's company.

Gemma and Gerald arrived just after lunch, and Gemma's gaze was derisive as it swept over Katy. Katy felt as if Gemma knew everything that had happened during her time with Adam, and colour flooded her cheeks, making her look guilty.

'Did you have a good time?' Gerald asked insinuatingly.

'Did you?' Adam returned smoothly, meeting Gerald's eyes head on.

'Er—yes, very good,' Gerald's gaze faltered and fell. 'You didn't meet up with us,' he added.

'Katy was ill,' Adam replied.

Gemma gave her a sharp look. 'Ill? What was wrong with you?'

A broken heart! 'Just a virus,' she answered quietly.

'As long as you can travel on the plane,' Gemma shrugged dismissively.

Adam pinpointed her with a narrow-eyed gaze. 'Katy was very ill for several days.' His tone left her in no doubt of his opinion of her attitude to her sister.

'Oh. I—— Are you feeling better?' Gemma asked her tightly.

'Much,' Katy almost smiled at the resentment in her sister's rebellious face. 'Adam looked after me very well.'

'I'll bet he did,' Gerald grinned, then his humour faded as he saw the look of cold anger in the other man's face. 'Very good of you,' he muttered.

'It was,' Katy agreed.

'I'll be off now,' Adam said briskly. 'Coming outside to see me off, Katy?'

'Yes,' she nodded eagerly.

'Goodbye,' Adam nodded curtly to the other couple.

Katy followed him outside, a feeling of desolation sweeping over her. She would never see him again, would never again know his arms about her, his lips on hers.

'Oh, Adam!' She threw herself into his arms, weeping on his shoulder.

'Hey,' he chided teasingly, 'I know your sister is a bitch, but she isn't that bad.'

She choked back the tears. 'That isn't why I'm crying.'

'I know,' he said gently. 'But it's all for the best. You'll soon forget me and——'

'Never!' she told him vehemently, perhaps revealing too much of her feelings, but in that moment not caring.

'I want you to, Katy. I'm a bastard of the first degree. I could only ever hurt you—I already have without meaning to.' He bent to kiss her briefly on the lips. 'Be happy, Katy. Have half a dozen kids and be happy. Promise me?'

'I——'

'Promise, Katy.'

'I can't,' she said tearfully, knowing she didn't ever want to get married if Adam wasn't to be her husband.

'Forget all about me and think of Andrew.' He kissed her softly, framing her face with his hands, his touch gentle. 'I'm sure if you give him a chance you'll find yourself married to him before the end of the year.'

'Adam, it's you I——'

'No!' He put his fingers firmly over her mouth. 'Don't say it. I can't handle those sort of emotions. It puts me under an obligation to you, and I can't take that.'

'All right,' she gave a wan smile, 'if that's the way you want it.'

'It is. Now go back to your secure little world and let me get on with being the swine I usually am. But I've enjoyed our time together, Katy. It's certainly never been dull!'

Gemma was alone when Katy went back inside the hotel. 'Gerald got fed up waiting,' she said crossly, jabbing her finger on to the lift button. 'What's that?' she indicated the small parcel in Katy's hand.

'It's a present.' The little jade bear hadn't left her since Adam had given it to her. 'From Adam,' she added softly.

'What is it?' Gemma demanded to know. 'Is that all?' she scorned once Katy had shown her. 'Two weeks of sleeping with Adam Wild and all you got out of it was that old bear,' she derided.

Katy had also got the biggest heartache of her young life, but she intended keeping that to herself. 'Adam and I have not been sleeping together,' she said stiffly.

'If I believed that I'd believe that pigs can fly,' Gemma scorned, 'and we both know they don't. Don't worry, Katy, I don't intend telling Mum and Dad about it. You keep quiet about Gerald and me sleeping together and I'll do the same for you.'

'You can tell Mum and Dad what you damn well please,' Katy told her angrily. 'I have nothing to hide.'

Gemma shrugged. 'Please yourself. But if it ever comes

out about you and him I know which story most people will believe.'

'You're disgusting!' And Katy left her.

England was cold, the eight weeks since their return making it even colder. The shops were starting to get their Christmas gifts in stock, but Katy could raise no enthusiasm for it.

She had settled back with her family quite quickly, although she knew she would never again be the naïve little girl who had set out so excitedly for Canada. She was a grown woman now, with an adult love for a man she could never have.

Gemma spent most of her time with Gerald, so Katy saw little of her. Not that she minded that, finding that when they did meet they only argued. Katy could see her sister for what she was now, a very selfish girl. She and Gerald should make an ideal couple.

Katy was ashamed of these feelings towards her sister, the sister she had always looked up to. But Gemma's behaviour in Canada had been so disgraceful that not even Katy could forgive her.

The little jade bear stood in a place of honour on the side unit in her bedroom, being the last thing she saw at night and the first thing she saw in the morning. She wondered if Adam had kept the wallet she had given him or whether he had put it to the back of a drawer and forgotten about it— and her. That would be the logical thing for him to do, unless of course he had disposed of it altogether.

She doubted he was back in the country yet, although she kept a watch in the newspapers for a report of his return.

'Would you come out to dinner with me tonight?'

Katy raised startled eyes from the notes she had been checking through, looking up into Andrew's good-looking face. 'What did you say?' she asked absently.

Andrew sighed, a tall handsome man of thirty, his blond good looks of a type that really didn't appeal to Katy, although she liked him immensely. 'Dinner, Katy,' he said patiently. 'I've asked you twice if you'll go out to dinner with me tonight.'

'Oh, I can't, Andrew,' she instantly refused, searching for an excuse that wouldn't hurt him. 'I—— We have my grandmother coming over for dinner this evening,' she said thankfully. 'She doesn't like it if all the family aren't there.'

'Oh,' he said dully. 'Is that the only reason? I've asked you out a lot the last few weeks, and each time you've refused. Oh, I know there've always been reasons for the refusal, but were they the real ones?'

'Of course they were,' Katy soothed, a pale reflection of herself. She had lost weight in the last eight weeks, and her face was unhealthily pale, her mouth unsmiling.

'You aren't looking well,' Andrew voiced critically. 'And I——' he broke off as someone came into the waiting-room.

'Good afternoon, Mrs Bennett,' Katy greeted the aged lady. 'What can I do for you?' She saw Andrew disappear back into his surgery, and smiled to herself. Mrs Bennett lived alone with her chair-ridden husband, and whenever she came to pick up his prescriptions she always stopped to have a chat. This was her own therapy; she loved a gossip with any available person who didn't manage to get away quick enough. Andrew had made good his escape before that happened.

'Just Bill's prescription, love.' She lowered her considerable weight into one of the chairs. 'It's a fair climb up that hill.'

The 'hill' was a slight incline in the road, but being overweight Mrs Bennett felt every inch of it. Andrew could have saved the old lady this walk by leaving the prescription on his rounds, but he thought she benefited more from the walk. She was a lady who refused to diet, took as little exercise as possible, and so Andrew used devious methods to help her. Not that she considered it help; she often grumbled about his inconsiderateness.

'Ah, here we are.' Katy drew out the prescription, handing it to the woman. 'Not long to Christmas now, Mrs Bennett,' she smiled.

'Can't abide it meself,' the woman replied taciturnly, her northern accent still with her despite her many years spent living in the south of England. 'All that money wasted on presents people neither want nor need.'

'Oh, but surely——'

'Bill and I always say as how it's madness. Never bought each other a Christmas present in our lives, and we've been married fifty years. It's all right for you young people with all your money, but Bill and I had to work years for the little we've got, and we certainly aren't going to waste it on such nonsense as *Christmas*.'

'I suppose not,' Katy found it easier to agree with the woman, knowing that Mrs Bennett preferred to do the talking while others listened. Poor Bill Bennett would have to sit and listen to all this conversation when his wife got home, would have the whole thing repeated to him word for word, full of 'And I said this' and 'I said that'. Katy's father had often said that he was surprised Bill Bennett hadn't murdered his wife years ago; certainly no one would have blamed him for it.

'No suppose about it,' Mrs Bennett said firmly. 'Christmas is a waste and that's the end of it. What I really wanted to know,' her voice lowered conspiratorially, 'is who the new tenant of Carstairs Manor is. I came by there just now and saw a removal van parked outside.'

Carstairs Manor stood at the other end of the village,

an old and gracious house, a house that looked as if it should be filled with children. It had been standing empty for the last year, since Lady Carstairs, the last owner, had died with no apparent heirs. A distant cousin had finally been traced in America and the house put on the market.

'And how would we know that, Mrs Bennett?' Katy asked interestedly. If this woman didn't know who was moving into Carstairs Manor then no one did.

'Well, they'd have to sign on here, wouldn't they?' the woman reasoned. 'Everyone needs a doctor.'

Katy didn't like to point out that anyone who could afford Carstairs Manor, a ten-bedroomed house, with servants' quarters attached, would probably also be able to afford private medical treatment. 'We've heard nothing, Mrs Bennett,' she told her truthfully.

'Oh. I heard it was one of those pop star people,' she added disgustedly. 'We don't want the likes of them around here.'

'I heard it was a film star,' Katy laughed. 'So I think we'll just have to wait and see.'

Mrs Bennett struggled to her feet. 'I think I'll just pop in and see May at the post office before I go home, she might have heard something.'

'She might,' Katy agreed. 'Mrs Bennett!' she hurried after her. 'You forgot your prescription.'

'Thank you, my dear, thank you. Was that Dr Maddox I saw in here talking to you a few minutes ago?'

Katy blushed. This woman didn't miss a thing! 'Yes,' she told her reluctantly.

'Nice young man.' Mrs Bennett looked at her knowingly. 'I suppose we'll be hearing wedding bells soon?' she said coyly.

'Not from me you won't,' Katy said stiffly.

'Hoity-toity!' the old woman muttered as she went out.

Andrew put his head round the side of the door minutes

later. 'Has she gone?'

'Yes,' Katy laughed at his hounded expression. 'And she's not at all happy about this pop star moving into Carstairs Manor.'

'I heard it was a millionaire who likes to live like a hermit,' he frowned. 'Oh well, what does it matter, you and I are having dinner together tonight.'

'I already told you——'

'I said we're having dinner together, Katy, I didn't say we would be alone. Your father has invited me to join you at your home.'

Dear Daddy, he meant well, seemingly the only person to notice she was no longer the happy carefree girl she used to be. He was worried about her, Katy knew that, and she wished she could put his mind at rest. But only Adam could make her happy, and there was no way she could have him.

Her grandmother was her usual domineering self that evening, demanding to know why Gemma and Gerald weren't married yet. 'High time you made an honest woman of her,' she told Gerald curtly.

'Mother!' Katy's mother was scandalised. 'The wedding is planned for next year, you know that.'

'Make sure you don't put the cart before the horse, young man,' Gerald was told firmly by the old lady.

Katy had to hide her smile. Her mother and father might be blind to the intimacy of Gemma and Gerald's relationship, but her grandmother missed very little with her piercing grey eyes. She was so delicate to look at, with her softly permed hair, rosebud and cream complexion, and her frail body, but the exterior hid a will of iron, and her tongue as sharp as a razor.

'And what's the matter with you, girl?' She turned on Katy now, wiping all humour off Katy's face. 'You look like a ghost. Not pregnant, are you?'

Katy heard her mother gasp once again. 'No, Grandmother,' she replied calmly, 'I'm not pregnant.'

'Mother, really——!' it was Katy's father's turn to protest now. 'Gemma and Katy are good girls. They would never——'

'Oh, don't be a fool, James,' his mother snapped. 'They may be good girls, but they're normal, aren't they? And Katy doesn't look well. She looks like I did when I was expecting you.'

James Harris began to look uncomfortable. 'Katy is just tired, she's been working too hard.'

'It isn't normal in a girl her age,' her grandmother remained adamant.

'I'm all right, Grandmother,' Katy said softly. 'As Daddy says, I'm tired.'

'What do you think, young man?' The old lady pinpointed Andrew in her gaze. 'She isn't well, is she?'

'She's a little run down, but I——'

'Why don't you ask her to marry you? She needs a man, that's what's the matter with her.'

Andrew coloured to the roots of his hair. 'I——'

'Shall we all go in to dinner?' Katy's mother stood up. 'It's all ready.'

'Don't you try and silence me, Eileen Harris,' the old lady snapped. 'I've known you since you were younger than Katy is, and I'll have my say!' Her voice was strident. 'Any fool can see that Katy is in love. I'm just trying to help things along.'

'Katy is perfectly capable of organising her own life, Mother.' James took her arm in a firm grasp and led her in to dinner.

Katy apologised to Andrew when they were alone later that evening. Her grandmother was irrepressible when in that mood, although she had behaved very well the rest of the evening.

'She's a wonderful old lady,' Andrew smiled.

'But so interfering. She loves arranging other people's lives for them.'

'Was she right?' Andrew asked gently.

'About my needing a man?' Katy taunted, watching hot colour flood his cheeks once again.

'No,' he said impatiently. 'Was she right about your being in love?'

'No.' She couldn't tell him the truth, not when it was another man she loved.

His shoulders slumped. 'Oh,' he sighed regretfully. 'I'd hoped . . . You know how I feel about you, Katy, must know that I'm in love with you.'

Yes, she knew. She had realised his feelings soon after her return from Canada—and had been trying to avoid a confrontation with him ever since. She didn't want to hurt him, she knew how painful unrequited love was, so she kept away from him whenever she could, refusing all his invitations to go out with him.

But she knew now that she couldn't avoid this situation any longer. 'I don't feel the same way,' she told him as gently as she could. 'I like you, I like you a lot, but it isn't enough.'

'You could learn to love me,' Andrew said eagerly. 'We've hardly been out together. We could——'

'I'm sorry, Andrew,' she interrupted firmly. 'But it wouldn't work.'

'Is there someone else?' He frowned. 'But there can't be, you don't see anyone else.'

'I'm afraid there is someone, Andrew,' she told him quietly. 'Someone I met some time ago. He—— He doesn't love me. He's probably forgotten my very existence by now.' Oh God, no! 'But I love him, and I—I'm afraid I always will.'

'But when—I don't understand when you met him.'

She had obviously taken him aback.

'It was a few months ago.' She didn't enlighten him any further. 'You don't know him. And I'm never likely to see him again.'

'Then if it's over——'

'Over!' she repeated ruefully. 'There was never anything to *be* over. No, that isn't strictly true. But it was over before it even began. I can't love you, Andrew, I'm sorry.'

He left shortly after that and she knew she had hurt him. But what else could she do? Oh, she could have lied to herself, could have let herself believe she could come to care for Andrew, but in reality she knew it wasn't even a possibility.

Gemma came into Katy's room just as she was getting into bed. 'Well? Did he ask you?'

'Ask me what?' Katy straightened the covers around her.

'To marry you, of course,' Gemma said impatiently, coming to sit beside her on the bed. 'Gerald says that Andrew's been after you for months.'

'What a typically disgusting Gerald remark,' Katy wrinkled her nose with distaste. 'And completely untrue.'

'You mean he *didn't* ask you to marry him?'

'No, he didn't.' She wasn't lying, he hadn't actually said the words, and this way it would save Andrew so much embarrassment.

'I could have sworn ... Oh well, he'll probably get around to it some time.'

'I don't think so. You see, even though he didn't ask me I made sure he would know I wouldn't accept even if he did ask.'

'My God, you didn't tell him about Adam Wild?'

Katy flushed. 'Not exactly.'

'What do you mean, not exactly?' Gemma stood up to

look down at her scornfully. 'Either you did tell him or you didn't.'

'I told him there was someone else.' Katy evaded her sister's eyes.

'And how!' Gemma laughed. 'You can tell me, is Adam Wild as good a lover as he's reputed to be?'

Katy's blush deepened. 'Gemma——'

'Oh, do tell me, Katy,' her sister encouraged eagerly. 'I've held my curiosity in check all these weeks, the least you can do is tell me now.'

'He was not my lover!' Katy snapped angrily.

'Oh, come on, Katy,' Gemma chided. 'You were with him all that time, you must have slept with him.'

'I didn't!'

'But he said——'

'He?' Katy interrupted sharply. 'You mean Adam?'

'Of course I mean Adam.'

Katy frowned. 'But when did he speak to you?'

'Don't you remember? It was that day after you decided to go off with him. He telephoned——'

'The day I decided——!' Katy gasped. 'I didn't *decide* anything, you left me to it. I believe your words were "He was welcome to me".'

'Only after he told me you would prefer to travel with him. I thought it was a damned cheek after Gerald and I had asked you along on our holiday.'

'I'm not understanding this,' Katy said uncertainly. 'Adam actually said I *wanted* to travel with him?'

'Well, of course he did. I may be a selfish little bitch, but even I wouldn't just desert you to a wolf like him. He told me you'd asked him if you could go with him. Faced with something like that I had no choice but to agree to you staying with him. But I was furious at the time.'

Katy was dazed. Adam had told Gemma she wanted to stay with him. But why?

CHAPTER TEN

It hadn't been too difficult to get the day off work; her father had agreed that a day's shopping in London was just what she needed. Her mother had taken over for her in the office, so there were no problems in that direction.

As soon as she reached London Katy dialled Adam's telephone number, a woman with a rather sexy voice answering her request for directions to the studio.

Katy had known after speaking to Gemma that she had to see Adam again, if only to find out why he had kept her with him when she needn't have been. Yesterday she had seen his name listed as one of the people present at a charity dinner, and so without giving herself time to think she had made the necessary arrangements to come to London.

She had plenty of time to think, on her way over to the studio, to wonder at her impetuosity. The receptionist had told her that Adam was in, but Katy had no way of knowing if he would see her.

The studio was what she would have expected, ultra-modern, the girl behind the desk completely compatible with her surroundings. She was a tall blonde, her make-up perfect, her dress impeccable; one of those sophisticated women Katy had accused Adam of surrounding himself with.

The woman turned from watering the many pots of greenery that stood about this outer office, a coolly polite smile on her face. 'Can I help you?'

Katy wasn't sure now. This environment, the sophistication of this woman, all made her realise that the Adam she came to know in Canada was not the same Adam who worked here. He had people working for him, was the top photographer of the country, and to think that their brief relationship still meant anything to him was highly unlikely. What she had told Andrew was probably right, Adam would have forgotten her existence.

'Can I help you?' the receptionist repeated.

'I—er—I——'

'Fiona darling!' A tall redheaded woman with bright red lipstick and very dark make-up breezed into the office, rudely pushing her way past Katy, the perfume she wore expensive and exclusive.

Katy stepped back. Not that she had any choice about it, she felt sure she would have been knocked over if she hadn't moved.

'Is he in?' The redhead arched an eyebrow in the direction of the inner office.

Katy had never seen anyone so exquisitely beautiful; she placed the woman's age at about thirty-five, possibly forty. She had long slender legs shown to advantage in the high-heeled sandals she wore, her slender figure complemented by the silky black dress Katy felt sure had an exclusive label in the back of it, her hands long and slender, the nails painted the same vivid red as her lipstick.

'He's busy at the moment,' Fiona answered calmly, apparently accustomed to such behaviour. She looked at the watch on her slender wrist. 'He should be finished in about ten minutes——'

'Oh, I can't wait,' she was told petulantly. 'I have to see Adam now, it's very important.' The redhead brushed past the receptionist.

'But you can't go in there!' The girl followed her. 'Mrs Wild, you can't go in there!'

'Don't be silly, Fiona,' the other woman snapped, opening the studio door. 'Ah, Adam, I——'

'What the hell do you want?' Katy heard him rasp, recognising his voice at once. 'I've told you before about interrupting my work. Whatever the problem is I don't have time to discuss it now—can't you see I'm busy?'

'You always are,' the woman dismissed. 'At home and here. Now I want to talk to you about the arrangements for this dinner party I'm to give for you.' The door closed behind her, cutting off the rest of the conversation.

Katy felt numb. That woman, that beautiful woman, was Adam's *wife*! In the ten weeks since they had parted in Canada Adam had married this woman. Not that it sounded as if it had mellowed him at all; his tone was harsh, his manner impatient.

'I'm sorry about that,' the receptionist sighed. 'What can I do to help you? Do you have an appointment with Mr Wild?'

'No. I—— That lady, she was Mrs Wild?' Katy just had to confirm that she hadn't misheard, that that really had been Adam's wife.

'Yes.' The girl held back her grimace. 'If you want to see Mr Wild I'm afraid you'll have to wait for a while.'

'No, I—I think I'll leave it,' Katy gave her a bright smile. 'Thank you, anyway.'

'But—your name!' the girl called after her. 'Can I have your name so that I can tell Mr Wild——'

'It isn't important,' Katy told her lightly, making good her escape.

Adam was married! There could be no other explanation, she knew he was an only child, so there was no possibility that the woman could be the wife of his brother. The woman had been beautiful, was perhaps a model, which was perhaps how Adam had first met her.

She had been the sort of wife Adam would choose, a woman who knew and appreciated his life-style, a woman so sure of her own beauty she had no need to worry about the women Adam photographed.

'Your day out doesn't seem to have done you any good,' her father frowned at her worriedly as she tidied his clinic-room for him later that evening. He was sitting at his desk writing up his notes at the end of his day. 'You're looking paler than ever.' He gave her his full attention, sitting back to watch her nervy movements. 'Are you sleeping, Katy?'

'Sometimes,' she told him wanly. 'I think it must be the changes in the weather, it's very depressing.'

'Don't be silly, Katy. You've been quiet and depressed since your holiday. Nothing happened over there, did it? Gemma didn't——'

'Gemma didn't do anything, Daddy,' she hastened to reassure him.

'Surely Gerald didn't——'

'Nor Gerald either,' Katy cut in firmly. 'I think I had such a good time that I can't get back into the swing of things.'

'Maybe that's it,' he accepted. 'Glad you went?'

'Oh, very glad. Canada was—it was breathtaking. All of it.'

'I'm glad,' her father smiled.

Katy made a concerted effort the next day to pull herself together. Adam was married and firmly out of her life, and she had to try and carry on without him now. When Andrew asked her out to dinner she agreed, and his pleasure almost made her feel guilty.

'You really will?' he asked eagerly.

'I really will,' she smiled. 'I'm looking forward to it.'

'So am—Oh no!' he groaned, his gaze fixed out of the window. 'Here comes Mrs Bennett. I'll see you later,' and he rushed into his office.

Katy laughed to herself, as she sorted the lab reports

into some order. She could hear Mrs Bennett's wheezy breath even before she had got through the door.

'Thank you, young man,' she said breathlessly. 'It's nice to know there are still some manners left in the younger generation.'

'Thank *you*—for placing me in the younger generation,' drawled a deeply familiar voice.

Katy looked up to see Adam holding the door open for Mrs Bennett to enter the waiting-room. Her face paled and the lab reports crumpled in her hand. Adam here! It seemed unbelievable, especially as only yesterday she had gone to see him. Surely it had to be a coincidence?

'Would you like to go first, young man?' Mrs Bennett offered. 'I usually take a while to get my breath back.' She eased herself down into her usual chair.

He gave his most charming smile. 'I'm only here to see Katy, so you go ahead.'

'Here to see Katy, are you?' Mrs Bennett said eagerly. 'Are you her young man?'

'Well, I——'

'You're a wicked old lady,' Katy scolded teasingly, speaking for the first time, her voice shaky. 'Mr Wild has just come to visit me.'

'Shame! He seems nice, Katy. You could certainly do worse.'

Colour flooded Katy's cheeks. 'Mr Wild is just a friend, Mrs Bennett.'

'Oh well,' she struggled to her feet, 'I suppose you want to talk in private.' She took the prescription Katy held out to her. 'I asked May about the new people at Carstairs Manor,' she said conspiratorially. 'She says they're moving in this week.'

'Oh yes?' Katy was too conscious of Adam to encourage the elderly lady in her usual chatter.

The brief glance she had dared to dart in Adam's direction had shown her that he had changed little; he was still lithe and attractive, the denims and sweater still as casual. Why was he here? How had he found her? The latter was the first question she asked him.

He shrugged. 'There are only three Doctor Harrises in the book for this area. I eliminated the other two and—well, here I am.'

'Why?'

His eyes narrowed, revealing fine lines beside his nose and eyes. He looked leaner too on closer inspection. 'You came to see me yesterday.'

Katy's startled gaze clashed with the calmness of his. 'How do you know that?'

He grinned, and was once again the old Adam, the Adam who made her heart ache. 'I only know one girl with caramel-coloured hair and grey eyes.'

She flushed. 'Your receptionist told you!'

'She did.' He took out the wallet she had bought him in Canada, producing a photograph of Katy from inside it. 'Showing her this confirmed it.' He sat on the edge of her desk.

His sudden nearness unnerved her. She hadn't even been aware of him taking that photograph. It was one of her standing beside Maligne Canyon—before she had fallen over and twisted her ankle. And Adam still had the wallet, he hadn't discarded it at all.

She looked down at her hands. 'And that sent you down here?'

'Fiona said you left in a hurry.'

She gave a forced light laugh. 'I was in a hurry, I had a train to catch. I only called in on the offchance. I was shopping in London.'

'Did you buy anything?' He picked up the paperweight from her desk and studied it.

'Buy any——? I—er—yes, I bought a—a new dress.'
Trust him to ask a question like that!

'Good.' He stood up. 'You can wear it tonight.'

'Tonight?' Katy echoed dazedly.

'Mm, when I take you out to dinner.'

'Dinner? I'm not going to dinner with you!'

'Is that any way to act when I took the trouble to come
here? Surely dinner isn't too much to ask?'

'You have no right to ask me out,' she told him resentfully. 'Anyway, I already have a date for tonight.'

Once again his eyes narrowed. 'With Andrew?'

Katy was surprised he had remembered the other man's
name. 'Yes,' she said abruptly.

'Are you going to marry him?'

'I might. My grandmother thinks I should.'

'Family approval,' Adam mused. 'But I have Mrs
Bennett's approval, doesn't that count for anything?'

She flushed. 'Mrs Bennett doesn't know the first thing
about you,' but she did, knew much more about him than
he realised.

'Katy——' Andrew came out of his office at that
moment, his bag in his hand. 'Sorry,' he smiled at Adam,
'I didn't realise you were busy. I'm just off on my rounds,
Katy.'

'This is Adam Wild, Andrew,' Katy had perforce to
introduce the two men. 'Adam, Andrew Maddox.'

'Nice to meet you.' Andrew shook hands. 'I'm afraid I
have to run. I'll be back about two, Katy. Goodbye,' he
nodded to the other man before leaving.

'So that's Andrew,' Adam said thoughtfully.

'Yes.' Katy glared at him, expecting criticism.

'Nice man,' he surprised her by saying. 'So you aren't
free for dinner tonight?'

'No,' she said tightly, knowing that if he had come to
her a week ago, even two days ago, she would have

dropped any plans she had that didn't include him. But not now, not now that she had seen his wife.

'Tomorrow?'

'Afraid not,' she shook her head. 'I'm visiting my grandmother,' she told him at his questioning look.

'I'll go with you. Then we'll see how your grandmother feels about me.' He walked to the door. 'What time shall I call for you?'

'Adam, you can't——'

'What time?' he repeated curtly.

'I don't——'

'I'll be here at seven o'clock.' He closed the door firmly behind him.

Once again he had just walked in and taken over her life, overriding her objections and simply telling her what she should do. And she had let him!

'Adam Wild,' Andrew remarked thoughtfully to Katy later that evening. 'Is he the man who did the supplement on the children starving——'

'Yes,' she confirmed tautly, vividly remembering the sleepless nights it had given him. After seeing the photographs she hadn't been surprised; they were horrific. No doubt his wife had now taken care of his sleeplessness. Katy almost groaned with the agony of imagining Adam in the other woman's arms.

Andrew stirred sugar into the late-night coffee she had prepared him. 'How did you meet him?'

Katy explained the meeting on the plane, omitting the rest of it. Andrew just wouldn't understand.

'Interesting chap?'

'Very,' she acknowledged awkwardly.

'Mm,' Andrew looked down at his cup. 'Is he working in the area?'

Katy shrugged. 'I don't know. He—er—he said he just thought he'd call in.'

Andrew looked up. 'He's the one, isn't he, Katy? The man you love.'

'I——'.

'Don't deny it,' he gently touched her hand. 'I could see it in your eyes. And he obviously hasn't forgotten you.'

'No,' she agreed dully.

By seven o'clock the next evening she was beginning to wish he had. Married or not, she just couldn't say no to Adam.

She had hoped to be able to open the door to him herself and make good her escape without having to introduce him to her parents, but at the last minute there was an emergency in the office, so she was delayed getting ready.

Adam was in the lounge talking to her parents when she came down at seven-fifteen, an Adam she had never seen before, the light grey suit and black shirt fitting him as if they were tailored on him. He looked handsome and distinguished, and it was obvious from the first that he had charmed her parents.

'Ready?' He stood up on her entrance, the look in his eyes showing his approval of the plum-coloured dress she wore.

'Yes, we should be on our way,' she agreed. 'Grandmother will be getting worried if we're late.'

'Watch out for her, son,' Katy's father warned Adam. 'My mother doesn't mince her words. She's blunt to the point of embarrassment.'

Adam's glance mocked Katy. 'So that's where you got it from,' he taunted her. 'I love your mother already,' he told James. 'Her honesty is one of Katy's most endearing qualities.'

After that Katy couldn't get him out of the house fast enough, her face bright red with embarrassment. Adam had implied that not only did he love her grandmother but that he loved *her* too. And she knew that wasn't true.

'Adam——'

'Direct me to your grandmother's, Katy.' He put the car into gear and accelerated out of the driveway.

The next few minutes were taken up with directions, the powerful sports car eating up the miles to her grandmother's. Her grandmother clung to her independence with a fiendish obstinacy, resisting all efforts to get her to move in with her son and his family, living in her tiny cottage surrounded by the knick-knacks she had collected through her long life.

Katy bit her lip as she stood waiting for Adam to lock the car. 'My grandmother——'

'Sounds like a woman I'm going to like,' he finished for her, taking her elbow and leading her to the cottage door. 'Do we go straight in?'

'Yes. But——'

'Come on, then.' He opened the door for her, pushing her inside.

Katy had telephoned to warn her grandmother she would be bringing a guest with her and watched the razor-sharp grey eyes level on Adam as they came into the living-room. The old lady looked him up and down, her gaze piercing.

'So you're the young man Katy's been pining away for,' came her opening comment.

Adam smiled, his most charming smile. 'I don't know—am I?'

'Oh, I think so,' Katy's grandmother told him. 'Sit down, sit down,' she said impatiently. 'You kept him a secret, young lady,' she reprimanded Katy. 'Not that I blame you. If I were forty years younger,' she smiled almost coyly, 'I'd be after him myself.'

Katy blushed to the roots of her hair. 'Grandmother!'

'If you have nothing better to do than trying to silence

me,' her grandmother snapped, 'you can go and make us all some coffee.'

Katy stood up reluctantly, knowing the words had been in the form of an order, and no one disobeyed an order from her grandmother.

'Well, go along, Katy,' she was told impatiently. 'I want to have a nice chat with Mr Wild.'

'Go on, Katy,' Adam endorsed her grandmother's command. 'I'm sure your grandmother and I can find plenty to talk about.'

That was what she was afraid of! Heavens, her grandmother could have told Adam her life story by the time she got back. She was in such a hurry to get back that she forgot the milk and had to go back and get it.

'Put her in a muddle, you have,' her grandmother smiled her enjoyment at Katy's embarrassment. 'Drink your coffee and take her away from here.'

Adam gave a throaty laugh. 'I knew I was going to love you.'

'It's Katy I want you to love,' she told him sternly.

'Grandmother!'

'Oh, do stop nagging, Katy, you're getting as strait-laced as your mother. If Adam is to be my grandson-in-law——'

'He isn't!' Katy almost screamed her protest. 'Grandmother, you can't——'

'Take her away and make love to her,' the old lady said with a sigh. 'Look at her, she's about to start protesting again. I'm sure you have your own way of silencing her.'

Adam grinned. 'I do. I've enjoyed meeting you. Your granddaughter is very like you.' He stood up.

'She was impossible!' Katy exploded when they finally got outside. 'And you encouraged her,' she accused.

'I loved her,' Adam chuckled. 'I hope I have her

strength of character at that age—I'm sure you will have.'

Katy's mouth set in mutinous silence, and she only spoke again when she realised they weren't going in the direction of her home. 'Where are you taking me?' she asked nervously.

'To my home.'

'Your home . . .?' she echoed. 'But I—I can't go there! London is miles away, and—and my parents will be worried if I'm late home.'

'We aren't going to London,' Adam informed her calmly. 'I no longer live in London.'

'Then where——' She broke off, realising the direction they were driving. 'Carstairs Manor!' she exclaimed. 'We're going to Carstairs Manor!'

He nodded. 'My home.'

'*You're* the new owner?'

'Mm. Mrs Bennett was right, the new owner did move in this week.'

So it wasn't a pop star, or a film star, *or* a hermit millionaire, it was a famous photographer. 'When?' Katy squeaked.

'Yesterday. But I bought the Manor weeks ago.'

'Why?'

He shrugged. 'To live in.'

'Your wife didn't look the type to like living in the country,' she said bitchily.

His eyebrows rose. 'My wife? You can explain that remark when we get inside.' He parked the car and led her into the graciously furnished manor, taking her through to the large lounge and closing the door firmly behind her. 'What wife?' he frowned, standing beside the fire, the flames lighting up the room.

'There's no need to pretend, Adam. I saw her at your studio yesterday. She was very beautiful.'

'My wife . . .?' He still looked puzzled. 'But I—— Wait a minute! Tall, red hair, very bossy?'

'Yes,' Katy acknowledged resentfully. Let him try and deny this! 'And I heard your receptionist call her Mrs Wild, so it's no use denying her existence. I bet she's upstairs right now.'

'She'd better not be,' he said grimly. 'You heard Fiona call her Mrs Wild because that's who she is. She's my mother, Katy.'

'Your *mother*?' she gasped. 'But she can't be! She was too young to be your mother,' she scorned.

'Nevertheless she is. It's amazing what the occasional face-lift and a visit to a health farm two or three times a year can do. My mother is fifty-seven and looks twenty years younger. She acts it too,' he added disgustedly. 'A couple of months ago she wanted to present me with a stepfather younger than I am. He took one look at me and ran.'

'She really is your mother?'

'Afraid so,' he nodded.

It seemed incredible. And wonderful too. Adam wasn't married after all! 'She's very beautiful,' Katy said dazedly.

'Yes. Actually I see her as little as possible. It just so happens she's arranging a dinner party for me, a dinner party at which I need her presence.'

'Yes, I heard her say she was.' Katy was still dazed, hardly able to take it in.

'For you and your parents,' he informed her softly.

She raised startled eyes, unable to read much from his expression in the flickering firelight, the rest of the room in darkness. 'For us?' she frowned. 'But why?'

'So we can all get to know one another.'

'Why?'

Adam moved restlessly, almost reluctant to answer her.

'It seems the logical thing to do,' he told her gruffly.

Her heart leapt hopefully. 'Adam . . .'

'It wasn't supposed to work out this way,' he growled, staring morosely down into the fire. 'I was supposed to walk away from you as I have every other woman.'

'But you did,' she reminded him softly.

'Did I?' He turned to look at her, his expression savage. 'Then why am I here? Why have I bought this house?'

'I don't know.' But she was hoping—oh, how she was hoping!

'I do,' Adam snapped. 'God, I thought I was so clever, so immune to women, using them and then discarding them at will. Then you came along with your tranquil grey eyes and taunting smile, with a habit of getting into every awkward situation going. Oh, I walked away from you, but I soon came back, and this time I wasn't walking, I was running.'

Katy's hope increased; she was hardly able to believe what he was telling her. 'When did you get back from Canada?' she asked.

'A few days after you.'

'But I thought you were staying on for the skiing?'

He scowled. 'I came back to look for a house.'

'This house.' She looked about her appreciatively.

'Do you like it?'

'I always have. I used to visit Lady Carstairs before she died. She was a wonderful old lady. I'm sure she would approve of the way you've furnished the Manor.'

'Do you approve?'

'I hardly think——'

'Do you?' he repeated harshly.

'I love it,' she told him shyly.

'Thank God for that,' he sighed. 'I bought this place for you. It seemed the sort of house you would like, and it's near your family.' He drew a deep breath. 'I bought the house, had the decorators fitting it out as I wanted, then I was going to move in and court you in the usual way. When you came to see me yesterday I began to hope the latter wouldn't be necessary, and that the love I'd told you to forget was still very much alive.' His look was rueful. 'I've never courted anyone, I'm not even sure I'd know where to start. Why did you come to see me, Katy?'

'I told you,' she was still unsure of him, no words of love had been mentioned by him, 'I was in London shopping.'

'And you didn't buy a damn thing, your father told me.'

'Oh!' Colour stained her cheeks and she avoided his eyes.

Adam left the side of the fire to slowly walk over to her, pulling her to her feet and into his arms. 'Why did you come to London?' he murmured into the hair at her temple. 'The real reason.'

'Gemma said——' she had trouble thinking straight with his lips caressing her in this way, 'she said you deliberately kept me with you in Canada.'

'Ah,' he nodded. 'She got round to telling you that, did she? And that brought you up to London?'

'I—I just wanted to ask you why you did it.'

'I would have thought that was obvious,' Adam gave a husky laugh. 'I'd already tried to get you into bed with me once, it must have been apparent that I wanted to sleep with you.'

'In that case, why didn't you?'

Adam gave a deep sigh. 'Because I couldn't treat you like just another of my women. Even then I knew you meant something special to me. I couldn't photograph you because I didn't want other men looking at you, ogling what I wanted. I—I love you, Katy.'

'Adam!' She looked up at him, her eyes glowing. 'Do you really mean that?'

'I mean it,' he said huskily, gently touching the silkiness of her long hair. 'I think I must have known it from the beginning, even on the plane. I thought I was glad to see the back of you, and yet when I accidentally chose to eat at the same hotel in Calgary that you were staying at I jumped at the chance of seeing you again. From that night on, after I'd kissed you, touched you, I was lost. You seemed to be haunting me. I decided to ask you to join me, get you out of my system. You turned me down, but when you turned up later that night I thought you were just like every other woman I knew, a token resistance and then the coy acceptance. When you made it clear it was a genuine mistake I knew I had to keep you with me anyway.'

'Why?'

'I'm not sure, maybe I wanted to try and prove you *were* like all the rest. But you weren't, and never have been. You once wanted to tell me how you feel about me and I stopped you, told you to go to Andrew. But you didn't, did you?'

'No,' she said huskily.

'Thank God! Tell me now, Katy,' he pleaded, 'do you love me?'

'So much!' There were tears in her eyes. 'So very much. But I never thought you——'

'I'm a cynical bastard,' Adam crushed her to him, 'but I knew as soon as I'd left you that I was in love with you. Hell, I knew before that. God, if you knew how I felt when you told me you'd been wandering around on your own at night. I could imagine you ripped to pieces by some grizzly, and I knew I wanted to protect you. That's something I've never experienced before either. I blew my top that day you put that ring on your finger, because it had been so much on my mind to do just that that I thought you might have guessed just how deep I was getting. I was terrified of you finding out, was determined not to let you know I loved you. I was deliberately cruel to you.'

'I know.'

He gave her a hard kiss on the lips. 'I'm sorry, darling. I stayed in Canada fighting my feelings for a few days, until Jud persuaded me I was doing no one any favours by being away from you, that I could even lose you. I came home, found out where you lived, bought this house, and was about to start my plan of action when Fiona told me you'd been to see me. From that moment on I thought of nothing but getting down here to see you. Will you marry me, Katy?'

'Marry you . . .?' she repeated dazedly. 'You mean *marriage*?'

'Your grandmother assured me she wouldn't stand for anything less,' he teased.

'You *told* her?'

He nodded. 'And your parents. They approve, all of them. Do you?'

'Oh, Adam!' Katy threw her arms about his throat. 'I love you so much!'

'Oh *God*, Katy,' he groaned into her hair, 'I need you—how I need you! I'm sick of just imagining you there in bed beside me so that I can sleep. I want the real you beside me, and I want that until the day I die. I want the gentleness of you, the fierceness of you, I just need *you*, Katy darling. Will you be my wife?'

'But you want to be free. You said you did.'

'With you I will be free—free to love you, free to desire you, free to possess you.' His voice had lowered huskily. 'Marry me?'

'Oh yes, yes!' She began kissing him and couldn't stop,

both of them swept away on a tide of desire that was at last allowed its own freedom.

After two months of marriage Katy didn't regret a moment of the time she had been Adam's wife, knowing that their love had deepened and strengthened.

Adam was in the shower now, the two of them having just returned from having dinner with her family. He came through from the bathroom, towelling his hair dry, but otherwise naked, the wonder of his body stirring her to passion as it usually did.

'What were you and your father whispering about tonight?' he asked, watching her as she brushed her hair.

Katy slowly turned to face him. 'We weren't whispering,' she evaded.

Adam's gaze sharpened. 'Secrets, Katy?'

'No, not really,' she said jerkily. 'At least, it won't be a secret much longer.'

He frowned. 'Are you going to tell me?'

She gave a choked laugh. 'I think I should. How would you feel about—about becoming a father?' She watched him anxiously.

His startled gaze ran down the slender length of her body. 'You mean——'

'Yes,' she confirmed shakily, 'I'm having your baby, Adam.'

'I knew there was something different about you,' he said slowly.

'Different?' Katy echoed sharply, remembering Adam's opinion of pregnant women. It was too soon, too soon, and she would lose him when she became huge and grotesque.

'God, I should have realised,' he murmured almost to himself.

'Realised what?' she asked almost shrilly.

'That you're more beautiful than ever,' he told her huskily, his eyes adoring. 'You're right, Katy, pregnant women *are* beautiful.'

'Oh, Adam,' she choked, 'I'm so glad you said that!' She returned the passion of his kiss. 'Your mother will be furious at being made a grandmother.'

'Damn my mother! I love the idea of being a father,' he murmured against her throat.

'There is just one thing, Adam,' she played with the silky hair on his chest.

He looked down at her anxiously. 'There's nothing wrong, is there, with you or the baby?'

'No,' she laughed.

'Then what is it?' His lips probed the hollows of her throat.

'I—er—I appear to be *three* months pregnant.'

'Three? But—The night I asked you to marry me!' Adam gave a husky laugh.

'It would seem so,' she admitted shyly. 'My biggest accident of all,' she groaned.

He swung her up into his arms. 'Our baby isn't an accident. You gave me complete pleasure from the first, you're the woman I thought never existed, the woman who's entertaining out of bed as well as in it. I'm glad our baby was conceived that night, Katy, really glad.'

'So am I.' She gazed up at the man she loved, would always love, and who would always love her, the man who understood her, who cherished her and cared for her. This was freedom.

Harlequin Plus

WHAT ARE HOT SPRINGS?

Thermal or hot springs are interesting phenomena occurring all over the world. The ancient Greeks and Romans enjoyed basking in their warmth, and in Europe it has been fashionable for centuries to visit hot springs for one's health. Thousands of aching bodies are immersed in these mineral-rich warm waters that bubble out of the earth.

Anyone encountering natural hot springs for the first time is bound to wonder how and why. To discover gurgling hot pools next to a cold mountain lake—as in Yellowstone Park, Wyoming—is mystifying, yet the explanation is fairly simple.

Hot springs are formed by surface water from rain or snow that, over a long period of time, penetrates deep into the earth until it reaches an area of hot molten rock. Then the water is quickly heated, and the resulting pressure causes it to rise rapidly through the easiest escape routes, such as faults and natural conduits in the earth's crust. Occasionally water escapes as hissing steam, so intense is the heat below. The mineral content of water from these springs varies as widely as the temperatures, which may be anywhere from tepid to boiling point.

Some of the most famous hot springs are at Bath and Harrogate in England, Baden-Baden and Wiesbaden in Germany, Saratoga Springs in New York and Hot Springs in Virginia. In Iceland the natural hot springs are put to very good use, providing hot water and central heating for many homes and buildings.

What readers say about Harlequin Romances

"I never enjoyed love stories until I started reading Harlequin books."

M.M.,* Three Rivers, Michigan

"Who ever would have thought that so much pleasure could be found in such a small package."

D.H., West Palm Beach, Florida

"Thank you for having the type of books that people can enjoy reading over and over again."

K.F., West Germany

"Security is having six new Harlequins on the shelf waiting to be read."

L.F., Newbury, California

*Names available on request